Elders on the Run

A short novel by

Zary Greer

Hardstone Publishing

Printed in the U.S.A.

"There is an art to flying, or rather a knack. The knack lies in learning how to throw yourself at the ground and miss."

Douglas Adams

CHAPTER ONE

They lived on a houseboat just outside of Phoenix, Arizona. The boat was approximately two hundred and fourteen miles from the sea, and approximately twenty miles from the nearest lake, river, or pond. Norton occasionally referred to it as a "yacht", and Chub enjoyed the fact that they had the only one in the neighborhood.

In contrast to the brick homes around it, their "yacht" was made of wood and had the appearance of an ark. Norton and Chub spent two long summers shaping it that way, not because they thought a flood was coming, but because they simply liked the look.

Elders on the Run

One morning, Norton stepped outside in his cheetah fur slippers to smoke a cigarette, his eyes squinting upon seeing a notice pinned to the door.

Mr. Kronowski,

The Lakewood Homeowners Association is holding a meeting on the 7th, at 6:00 p.m. We will be meeting to discuss how your property stands in regards to neighborhood zoning regulations.

You are encouraged to attend.

Sincerely,
Thomas Johnson
President of the HOA

Norton left the notice there. He then took a drag from his cigarette and recalled a past conversation with his neighbor, Mr. Blaine.

"That damn boats a neighborhood disgrace," said Mr. Blaine, spit shooting out of his mouth.

"It is a grace," said Norton. "A real beauty."

"I said it's a disgrace you idiot! A disgrace!"

Norton knew the comment was true. The wood that he and Chub had used to shape the boat into an ark was pulled from an abandoned barn on Fourth Street. Norton recalled driving by as the construction crew was tearing it down. They gave him the wood with happy faces and watched gladly as he drove off, saving them a trip to the dump yard.

Norton first realized the boat might be a problem when

he tried to apply for a line of credit. The appraiser stopped in front

of the mailbox and looked twice at the address. Built on merely

one quarter of an acre, the lot was small. A few cacti popped up

from the ground in different places. A rusty trailer with flat tires

held the boat off the desert floor. There was a satellite dish

strapped to the bow of the ark and an old cable antenna that

teetered crookedly into the sky.

The appraiser took a deep breath as if to say, "I guess

this is it".

He then walked up to the boat.

Norton answered the door in his bathrobe and, thinking it

necessary to point out, stated his house was the only one in the

neighborhood with amphibious capabilities. The appraiser politely mentioned that the boat could not be considered a house, then

explained why he might wish to take out a loan against the land

instead.

"Listen," Norton said, "It's a houseboat. Key word

house."

"Listen," the appraiser said, "It's a houseboat. Key word

boat."

"You can't see the beauty in the Mona Lisa either, can

you?"

"What do you mean?" the appraiser asked.

"You're a moron" said Norton. "This '*boat*', as you call

it, has a fridge and an AC and a couch and even a toaster oven."

Norton really believed his boat would qualify as a home.

He could still remember the way the appraiser laughed, his tone so

condescending and reproachful, his smile smug yet oddly amused.

I need a vacation, Norton thought. He had woken up

late, and the sun loomed high above the horizon. A car full of

youngsters could be heard coming down the street, the speakers in

their car making a rhythmic *thump.*

Norton spit into the dirt. *Them again?*

When the Impala got close, Norton could hear the

suspension as the driver mashed the hydraulics, *uhyerr, uhyerr.*

The car bounced. A thug situated in the passenger seat hung out

the window and threw an egg into Norton's mailbox. Yellow

splatter erupted from white shards of shell, and, in retaliation,

Norton launched his ashtray with a side-armed sling.

"For Pete's sake, the old man's got an arm!" cried one of the boys from the backseat. The ashtray had flown from Norton's arm in a flash, smashing into the trunk of the car.

"We'll be back, Kranowski!" the driver yelled, tires peeling beneath him.

"And I'll be waiting!" Norton hollered back, his arm curled and fist shaking.

Norton stamped his cigarette out forcefully, the end crumbling under his fingers on the porch handrail. He walked back inside.

"What was all the ruckus?" Chub asked.

"The Winslow boys, again," said Norton.

Chub looked up. "You know, I thought this would be a quiet neighborhood when we moved in."

Norton and Chub had been having turf battles with the teens since March. Right when Norton thought he held a monopoly for hand-rolled cigarettes, the eldest Winslow boy began rolling some of his own. Norton and Chub were no match for the ambitious teenagers. A sign Norton had out in the yard, '*Cheap cigarettes: 45 dollars per carton'*, had mysteriously gone missing two months prior. Coincidentally, this was around the time those Winslow boys started working the corners. Norton and Chub could hardly compete. Their territory had been taken over.

"Watcha say we drive to Jaivon's BBQ Shack?", Norton asked Chub. "I think we need a day off."

Chub was pulling a packet of pancake batter out of a cabinet. Hesitantly, he put it back up.

"I guess barbeque sounds okay."

"Ah, the Kranowskis," said Jaivon, as Norton and Chub

pulled up. "Put another slab of meat on the smoker, son. That big

one likes to eat."

The truck let out a squeal when it came to a stop. A puff

of gray smoke coughed out of the tailpipe and went up in a plume.

It was the last of the T-Line models still on the road, all the others

having long since met the junkyard. A good thing kids don't judge

an ice cream truck by its age.

Norton and Chub always wore red aprons if they were

working, the words *'Grandpa Scoops'* embroidered in white across

the chest. The previous owner had mounted a neon sign to the roof that said, '*Keep Chillen*'. Norton had tried taking the sign off, but a broken wrench and five bruised knuckles later, '*Keep Chillen*' became their slogan.

On a chalkboard below the service window, a listing of fifteen different ice creams were written in barely legible handwriting, everything from snow cones and rainbow dots to drumsticks and pop-ups. The truck now found itself rusted and sitting on a full set of donut tires because, as Norton liked to say, "Why store up a good tire?"

When the two entered the restaurant, Javion gave them a jovial shout.

"Gentlemen, things going alright?"

"Another day," said Norton, "nothing new."

"You want the usual?"

"Please."

A thick-bodied smell of oaks and caramels filled the air. Jaivon's quaint shack was made of dark wood and overlooked a Walmart parking lot. Norton and Chub enjoyed watching people enter and leave. Sometimes they even sold ice cream there.

"Come get your barbeque and ice cream!" they would broadcast through the loudspeaker. Norton and Chub were the only ones who thought those two things went together, but people would come nonetheless, for one or the other.

"Gonna be doing any work today?" Jaivon asked.

"No," said Norton, "I think we've earned a day or two off."

Norton then proceeded to quarrel with Chub for choosing to sit down at the table with wobbly seats. He always hated the table with wobbly seats.

When the meal was brought out, Chub grabbed two handfuls of napkins. Norton figured he would be grabbing more by the time he finished. Steam wisped up from their sandwiches. Norton spit his bubble gum into the parking lot and Chub watched as it rolled to a stop.

"Got me a new smoker," said Jaivon. "Investment, you know? Tough to keep the business going if you don't invest."

"Smells good for once," said Norton, swallowing his first bite.

"I've three extra feet of rack. And a metal box to keep my cookware too. You fellas should step around back and see it when you're done!"

Three orders of french fries and an extra sandwich later, Chub stopped requesting more food. Jaivon's new smoker was clean, unlike the old one, which had grease fat oozing from the seams. Chub gave his compliments. Norton simply squinted.

"I wonder why we haven't heard from Duffy lately," Chub said as they were leaving.

Norton pulled out his cellphone. "Why don't we call him?"

Chub watched his brother patiently. A few seconds passed and Duffy finally answered. Norton exchanged greetings and Chub waited as Duffy spoke on the other end of the line.

"Okay," said Norton, "Greenville Park? Me and Chub will head there... See you then."

Norton pulled into Greenville Park with more speed than he knew how to control. Such was always the method of his driving. Chub braced his legs into the floor as his side of the truck rode up onto the curb before halting violently. A woman gazed up from the spot next to them, her jaw gaping at the unexpected hunk of tonnage now towering over her car.

"Little dogs annoy me," said Norton, referring to the dogs in the backseat of the woman's car, yapping away madly, teeth bared at the monstrosity beside them.

The two slid out of the doorless truck. Chub thought of how much he liked driving a vehicle that let in the wind. Norton jerked his foot to the side, dodging a wet piece of a bubble gum.

"People," he said, his voice holding disdain for the person who spit it out.

Off in the distance, they could see their friend Duffy. He was in the process of stretching out a large, yellow canvas. Norton and Chub wondered what he might be up to, but they had a general idea.

"Watch out for that—" Chub tried to warn Norton, but it was too late. A quartet of flies hovered around a light brown mush stuck to the side of Norton's shoe. Chub immediately smelled the stench and felt grateful, typically he was the one stepping in shit.

"Keep walking," said Norton, his tone disgruntled, as though Chub himself had placed the shit there.

"What do you think?" Duffy asked when Norton and Chub were close, his arms stretched out towards the canvas.

Norton and Chub were staring at a hot air balloon that was painted vibrant yellow, a large smiley face drawn across its center. Norton and Chub cracked a pair of grins.

"They say smiles are contagious," said Duffy. "I can't wait to get a picture of it up in the sky. I've already scheduled a date with a photographer. Friend of mine said he's the best in town."

Chub wondered when he might have a chance to go up with Duffy. He and Norton had been up with Duffy before. They often thought fondly of their skyward adventures.

"I'm glad you two rode out. I could actually use some help. Got a good deal for the balloon off eBay. It did have a hole that needed to be patched, though. That's what I'm doing now. If one of you would hold the fabric right here." Duffy was bending down with a fairly big sewing needle and some yellow string.

Chub volunteered and pulled a stretch of fabric taut so that Duffy

could easily sew in a seam. While waiting, Norton cursed off to the

side in the grass, a Swiss Army knife in his hand, whittling at the

poo wedged into the creases of his shoe.

"This time next year," said Duffy, "I'm thinking about

joining the Frankfurt Air Race League. Last year the series started

in Maine but there's talk of starting it in Texas next year. The

number of balloons varies from race to race, but there are typically

over one hundred competitors at each event. Prizes for first place

start at six grand. If you win the whole series, you win an

additional fifty."

Chub looked at Duffy with beaming eyes. Norton stopped plucking away at the bottom of his shoe and gazed up for a second. He then resumed his business and Duffy continued.

"It can be dangerous, of course. They hold the events regardless of the weather conditions. Last year at the main event in Oregon, two balloons collided, one got wrapped around a cell phone tower and another had to land in the middle of a lake." He paused, "I'm going to have to get a better engine, between now and then, if I'm to have any chance at winning."

"Does it cost anything to enter?" Norton asked.

"All you have to pay for is race insurance," said Duffy, "Insurance on your engine. That's all it is really. They want to make sure people aren't going up with something like, well—what I have now."

Norton and Chub looked askance.

"What do you mean—something like what you have now?" Norton asked, thinking of their last balloon ride.

"The engine is just old," said Duffy, "That's all. Companies won't insure an old engine. She runs like she should. Hot air balloons don't fall like a helicopter when their engine gives out anyway. They only do that if they rupture."

"Which is exactly what the balloon you just bought did," said Norton, gesturing toward the patch Duffy and Chub were sowing.

Duffy gave Norton a wink. "I think that's it. Just one more stitch here."

"Should be fun dying with—I mean flying with ya" said Norton.

They all smiled, as though the additional risk only added to the adventure. Norton and Chub then helped Duffy roll up the balloon. They folded three ends inward and walked toward each other. Duffy kept telling Chub to stop stepping on the balloon and Norton began explaining why Chub was an idiot. A group of onlookers had stopped to watch the commotion, wondering what the three were doing and why they were arguing. Chub waved at them, dropping his end of the balloon, but, eventually, the three managed to fold the behemoth into a neatly packed square.

It took all they could do to carry the heavy nylon canvas over to Duffy's truck. Norton and Chub wondered how Duffy had managed to get it out on his own. They always wondered about the little things Duffy would do. He was a man of mystery, an enigma, always up to something and normally something far from ordinary.

Duffy never bothered with mundane things. He was a good friend to Norton and Chub. Their personalities complemented each other nicely. Duffy was easy-going and mysterious enough to gain Norton's respect, but he was also kind enough to value Chub's opinions, something Chub's brother would rarely, if ever, do. Perhaps more importantly, though, was the fact that if they ever needed anything, Duffy was there.

After they loaded the balloon into the truck, Duffy thanked them. He told them he would be in touch the next time he went out. They then watched as Duffy drove off and left the parking lot. When the truck was out of sight, Chub asked Norton the question that had been on his mind since they left the BBQ Shack: namely, what would be for dinner?

"We don't have any money," said Norton, "and we owe

the Homeowners Association twelve months' dues."

"Well," said Chub glumly, "do we have enough for root

beers?"

Norton thought about it for a second. He sighed, "We

have enough for root beers and a tub of worms."

*****

Their fishing spot was located a good drive north of

Phoenix on the Salt River. They had to carry their coolers and

tackle off the road about half a mile. The eddy they fished in was

small, but Norton was certain they had the best spot in Arizona.

Chub always protested the walk there and regretted the walk back, but he didn't care too much for the crowds at popular spots.

When they arrived their seats were still waiting where they left them from the last time. Norton pulled a bottle opener out of his pocket. After popping the top on his root beer, he handed the opener to Chub. Making a wish for good fishing, they threw their bottle tops into the water.

Norton slid a brass spoon onto his line. He then tied a Palomar knot around a small spinnerbait. Giving his pole a cast, Norton's reel made a zipping sound as the line unraveled. The bait hit the water with a *kaplump!*

Chub rigged his pole with a one-ounce sinker, a bobber, two worms, and then another two worms to be sure. He dropped his line and sat back to savor his soda. He was more of a sit and

watch the pole kind of guy.

Without much wait, the tip of Norton's pole jerked

downward and his reel began to whine. He tilted his rod down then

slowly lifted up again. Repeating this motion, Norton played a

game of give and take with the fish, careful not to pull too hard and

pop his line. "It's a good one. Grab the net," he said breathlessly.

Chub scooped low into the water but the fish managed to

evade him. He tried again, this time successfully.

"A nice start!" said Norton, energized by the catch.

Chub held the fish up to look at its size. "Three pounds

easy," he said, placing the bass into their cooler. The two fished

until the last of the stars were out.

"We'd better go now," said Norton eventually. Chub, of course, was genuinely hungry at this point. By the time they had made it back, he could barely stand the wait as they cleaned the fish from the stern of their boat. His stomach rumbled, but he was happy, nonetheless. In their quaint and quiet neighborhood, with their catch spread out across the back, the boys looked like they had just pulled into harbor after a long day and a good haul.

Yet despite this cause for happiness, Norton couldn't help but think about the notice on the door. He wondered how many more nights like this they would have.

CHAPTER TWO

"Hurry up," said Chub, as he slipped into a pair of boots that he'd bought from a military surplus shop, "we're going to be late. Last time we missed the line up and had to watch. I don't want that to happen again. They need me, Norton. I'm the one hoisting the flag at the opening ceremony!"

"Calm down, we're not going to be late."

Chub held a newspaper clipping in his hand.

'Come join us at Fort Verde for a special presentation with

Indian War period reenactors! July 7th,

8am-1pm'

He looked at the clock above the wall: it read 7:05.

"We've an hour's drive," he protested.

"We're leaving now," said Norton, donning an old blue

military coat accented with gold buttons. He grabbed his officer's

cap off the rack by the door, and Chub leapt from the couch.

Norton stopped on their starboard side porch. "Forward. March!"

he exclaimed, and the two marched down from the houseboat in

step.

Chub hopped into the passenger seat as Norton undid the

positive and negative terminals running from the battery charger.

Flipping a switch, he turned the charger off and closed the hood of their truck. "We really need a new battery," said Norton as they

pulled out of the drive, "I'm tired of having to connect it to the

charger every night."

As the two backed out of the driveway, Norton noticed

the Winslows four houses down. He could almost feel his blood

pressure rising. The eldest was hanging out of his Impala and

selling a pack of cigarettes.

"Mr. Hayes is our customer!"

"No," said Chub, "just let it go."

"You mean bend over? Is that what you expect me to

do?" Norton whipped the ice cream truck into the road.

"They're just kids, Norton. Just kids."

"Kids nearly dead. This is our neighborhood, Chub. Our

neighborhood!"

Seeing the ice cream truck rush into view, the eldest sped off in a terror. "Thanks, Mr. Hayes!" he said out the window as the car hurried off. Norton and Chub were coming fast. A ram from the old T-Line would put his Impala in the dirt. He was unsure if Mr. Kranowski would do such a thing, but he really didn't feel like learning. Norton blew past Mr. Hayes in a blur. Shocked and disoriented, Mr. Hayes nearly lost his balance in an attempt to get out of the way.

"The old man's crazy," yelled one of the boys from the backseat. "He was trying to hit us!"

Making a swift turn up one of the side streets, the Winslows sped off.

"This is embarrassing," said Norton, cursing his ice cream truck for being so cumbersome. He took the turn as fast as he could. Yet the truck was slow to get back up to speed.

"Cop!" yelled Chub, pointing out of the window. A white car had caught Norton's attention. He abruptly slammed on the brakes as the blue lights flashed brightly. To Chub's surprise, the cop never saw them.

Quickly getting out of his car and approaching the Impala, the officer gripped his side arm and spit into the dirt. Norton drove by slowly and gave a smug smile to the glum-faced teenagers. "They're selling cigarettes, sir! Bunch of thugs!"

The officer shot a look of contempt towards Norton, his brow ridge tightened and his gaze demeaning.

"Today's going to be a good day, Chub. You see that? That's karma see? Momma always said the universe works in mysterious ways. She was right, I say. She was right. Those kids had it coming."

"Maybe they're just trying to make it like us . . ."

"They've got allowances, Chub. Allowances. When is the last time you had an allowance?"

"Well . . . I guess it's been—"

"Exactly, Chub. Exactly."

As the two left the neighborhood and pulled onto the Interstate, Norton noticed Chub looking down at the clock on the radio. "It's okay, Chub. They're not going to start without us. Here, look at this. Duffy gave it to me yesterday in the park."

Chub found himself looking down at a vibrantly colored magazine, *Up, Up and Away!* it read across the title. Chub, with his eyes glazed over in awe of the balloons, flipped to an article titled *"Full of Hot Air!"*

"You like that?" Norton asked. "In the back, they have the classifieds, different balloons at different prices. I like the one on page 56. The blue one."

Norton was making a lane change, cutting off a young mother without realizing it.

"Wow," said Chub. "If we ever get that cabin in the Alps or that hut in Bali, imagine what the view would be like?"

"Oh, it would be amazing, Chub. I'm leaning towards Bali over the Alps. The winds are more forgiving. Just have to plan it right. Don't want to land in the ocean. Think about the money, though? What tourist wouldn't want to take a balloon ride in Bali? Imagine the view. A honeymoon ride over the Indonesian Islands, that must be pricey!"

Chub recalled Norton telling Duffy about the idea.

"I'd never launch from Bali or the Swedish Alps," Duffy advised. "Misjudge the wind and you're dead."

Chub was smart enough to know these words might be true. Even so, he never questioned Norton. After all, Norton had looked after him for his entire life. To think that Norton would get him killed, even though Norton had come close many times, was a thought Chub never entertained. In Chub's mind, Norton always knew what best to do. Getting the ice cream truck, that was Norton's idea, and Chub thought it a rather good one. However meagerly, the old truck had supported them for some time now.

They didn't work for anyone, and they had their own business.

They were proud of that.

When the two finally pulled into the park, Norton's

mind was running frantically over the Winslow incident, while

Chub was still nervous about being late. A bead of sweat swelled

from a pore above Chub's temple. He had never participated in the

flag-raising ceremony, and he knew everyone would be watching.

Norton, noticing Chub's nervousness, reminded him on how to

raise the flag as they entered the parking lot.

"Fort Verde is located near the Verde River, from which

it acquired its name. The park boasts three historic house museums

and a parade field."

As Norton and Chub got out of their truck, they could

hear a park ranger describing the site.

"From 1860 until 1866, a group of predominantly

Mexican recruits volunteered to live here and protect the settlers."

The ranger was talking to a small audience that seemed

to be paying no attention. Every one of their heads turned towards

the ice cream truck.

A woman looked to her husband. "Honey, how much did

we pay for this?"

"It's good for the kids," her husband said. "This is

history."

The Park Ranger continued, "From 1866 until the fort

was decommissioned, the U.S. Army occupied the compound.

Before the camp was resettled in 1871, there were 22 buildings

around a parade ground like this one. I'm sure you can only

imagine the fierceness with which the Indians fought if it required that many men to keep them at bay. But the Indians were not the

only thing the men had to contend with. In 1870, a bout of malaria

ravaged the camp. It is then that the camp resettled to where we

stand now."

Norton and Chub hurried into their positions while the

ranger was talking. He had been trying to delay the

commencement of the ceremony long enough for Norton and Chub

to take their spots. When Chub finally made it to the base of the

flagpole, the ranger gestured over at the trumpeter and signaled for

him to begin with taps. The re-enactors stood at attention with their

right hand in salute. Chub untied the cord that was wrapped around

a hook protruding from the flagpole and began to pull the flag

upward to the top. He then tied it off and resumed his salute until

the finishing of taps.

When noon rolled around all of the re-enactors assembled in a mess hall, their humdrum faces over plates of food. Here, in front of the onlookers, they told scripted stories and spread rumors of an Indian uprising. "We'll need to prepare the cannons," said Norton, intentionally adding coarseness to his voice for theatrical effect.

"I'll prepare the horses," said Chub, and the rest of the men escalated the story accordingly.

The kids in the group got closer to their parents and observed the scene intently, before the group was brought outside and onto the parade field. An alarm rang out, and a band of Indians poured from behind a building. They let out a wavering and high-pitched battle howl.

"Ready. Aim. Fire!" yelled an army trooper from the south side of the lawn. A cannon boomed. A shock wave rushed across the field. Indians collapsed but there was no explosion. Smoke from the cannon filled the air, wafted away by the wind. Army soldiers loaded their muskets and marched through the thinning cloud of white. Their guns let out a loud bang, and a few more Indians collapsed to the ground. The Indians left encircled the soldiers, each beginning to meet their end by bayonet. Chub was tasked with taking out one of the Indians, but he tripped on his shoelaces before reaching him and chose to play dead instead.

Shouts could then be heard from behind the crowd of spectators and, turning around, the onlookers witnessed doctors and surgeons run out into the field to mend the wounded. This whole show lasted another five minutes, but the event was soon over, and the soldiers fell back into formation. A soft and measly

applause emanated from the crowd before they were carried off to

continue their tour.

On the way home, Chub felt sad.

"I wish I played one of the Indians," he told Norton.

"We took their land. It's not right."

"No, it's not," said Norton. He then used the opportunity

to tell Chub about the notice pinned to their door. "Chub, we have

to go to a meeting tonight and fight for our home. Kind of like the

Indians did. Our neighbor, Mr. Blaine, has stirred up the

homeowners association. No one but me and you believe the boat

is a home. They're saying it breaks a zoning restriction."

"But the boat is a home," said Chub. "We live there."

*****

Norton and Chub walked into the building. Mr. Blaine

was standing behind a podium with roughly twelve homeowners

before him.

"Stop right there!' Norton yelled out, stomping his way

into the room.

Mr. Blaine muttered under his breath, "I told them we

shouldn't put a notice on his door."

"I believe I have a right to speak," said Norton.

Mr. Blaine proceeded calmly, "We haven't even started

yet, Norton."

"Good. You can all go home now. Meeting over. Thank

you for coming."

"Have a seat, please. There will be ample chance for you to make your case."

"I prefer to stand."

"Me, too," said Chub, chest puffed.

"As you all know, the Kranowskis own lot 121."

"You got that right," Norton interjected, "We own it! It's ours!"

"But," Mr. Blaine went on, "the home in question, I mean . . . that thing they made into a dwelling is . . ."

"It's a houseboat." Norton shouted, "Keyword *'house'!'*"

Everyone in the room could see Mr. Blaine turning red.

A woman from the back of the room stood up to express her opinion. "This whole situation is a shame," she started. "I would hate to see these two gentlemen go through any trouble, but the boat brings the value of our neighborhood down. It's one of the first things you see when you pull into the neighborhood."

Another man from the middle of the room spoke up, shaking his cane in the air. "That boat is on a trailer. Tow it away!"

"I think not!" said Norton, staring through the man.

"Everyone settle down," said Mr. Blaine. "I have asked Jake Cortell to join us this evening. Mr. Cortell, for those of you who haven't met him yet, is a property attorney." He let his hand out towards a gentleman in the front row, "Mr. Cortell?"

"Right, yes." The attorney got up and assumed the podium. "In the zoning regulations for this neighborhood, a home is defined as a permanently fixed structure." He looked towards Norton and Chub. "I believe, as one of your neighbors has already stated, your boat is on a trailer?"

"Been that way for years," said Norton, "before any of these fools moved in. I was one of the first people to buy a lot in this neighborhood. If they didn't want to live by my boat, they shouldn't have bought a house next to it." Norton and Chub truly were one of the first to buy a lot. They both remembered when they had practically the whole neighborhood to themselves.

The attorney smiled, "I've also had the chance to look over your association dues, Mr. Kranowski. You are more than twelve months behind on your payments. According to bylaws, this makes your property subject to foreclosure."

"I bet we're not the only ones behind on dues," said Norton.

"No, Mr. Kranowski, you're not. But you are the only ones behind by twelve months, and that is why you're the only ones subject to foreclosure. Tomorrow, I will be adding yet another

notice to your door. You'll have thirty days to make good on your

payments."

CHAPTER THREE

Chub worked on his fourth Choco Taco since noon, his mind ruminating over why they had never worked in a school parking lot before. They were waiting on the clock to hit 3:15, a moment at which children would stream out with untied shoelaces and backpacks in tow.

"Chub," Norton had said the night before, "we need to come by a lot of money. If we don't they're going to take our home. I've been thinking this over, and I can picture no place with more children than an elementary school. If there's ice cream to be sold, I believe that's where we'll sell the most of it."

They arrived early.

"This kind of feels like a stake out . . ." said Norton, flicking his cigarette out the window. "I'm not sure I like it."

"You should lay off those," said Chub. "They're going to kill you . . . and you know it. I just don't understand."

"Shut up and eat your ice cream." Norton paused for a brief moment, "Our old man smoked until he was ninety. Suppose I will too."

Chub's face suddenly held curiosity. "Hey Norton?"

"Yeah?"

"When do you think we'll have enough money to buy our balloon?"

Norton scratched his head. He and Chub had been planning to buy their own hot air balloon by the end of the year, but Norton knew the balloon was now much further off. "Maybe next year . . ." he said, knowing full well it would be at-least two years. Their net profit margin was barely enough to sustain the business. Twenty cents here. Twenty cents there. Just that morning, he'd used the previous month's profits to buy a new alternator. The original plan, now a lost hope, was to branch out, start a franchise, get more ice cream trucks. "There's gold in that rust bucket," said Norton on the day they bought the old T-Line. They were standing in a junkyard. That was two years ago. Now they were on the verge of losing their home.

"It's okay," said Chub, his lips covered in Choco Taco.

"Here. Wipe your mouth off." Norton handed him some paper napkins.

"Was somethin' else," said Chub, still talking about their last trip with Duffy. "I felt like a cloud, floatin' there with 'em."

"Guys will shell out for a proposal in one of these things," Duffy had told Norton six months earlier. The idea had been in Norton's mind since.

"Oh!"

"Oh, what?" said Norton, wobbling back in his seat, taken off guard.

Chub pointed with his right hand, his left spread out over his forehead in a look of disbelief. Norton turned to look where he was pointing.

"Norton!" Chub exclaimed. "Your cigarette!"

The shrubbery to the right of the truck was ablaze and a stream of red was glowing its way towards the school. Norton slapped his hand over his forehead, mirroring Chub's behavior, his jaw jutted outward. They stood there for a brief moment before Norton started pacing around in the truck. "Think," he said out-loud. "Think."

About this time, the fire had reached the building, burning at a faster rate than either of the two could think. Norton stopped and stood there again, "Could I have? Could I have set the school on fire?" The sound of a fire alarm suddenly rang out across the parking lot. "I . . . I . . . I've set the school on fire!" he exclaimed.

Norton looked to Chub for an answer. All Chub could do

was jump up and down frantically, "Think, Norton! Think!"

This time, Norton did think. He had positioned himself in

the driver's seat and slammed the truck into gear. Reality hit Chub

hard when his head collided with the scoop rack. He then hurried

himself to the passenger seat, oblivious to the throbbing pain above

his right ear.

As they rounded the parking lot, Chub looked out the

mirror and could see children rushing from the building. Teachers

ran around madly and shouted things he couldn't hear. A column

of black smoke billowed into the sky.

For whatever reason, Norton decided the quickest

getaway would be to ride across the median, cross a neighboring cow pasture, and head up the down ramp coming off of Interstate 35.

"Close your eyes," said Norton! The old T Line was plowing through some poor farmers' cattle. But it was too late. Chub had witnessed it all.

And sadly, this particular route might have worked, that is, had Norton been able to dodge the bright green Volkswagen after making it onto the interstate. The ice cream truck and the beetle made for a colorful collision. Klondike bars and rainbow cones catapulted out of the freezers, splattering onto the dash and roadside below. They sideswiped each other, almost hitting head on, but this put the truck at an awkward angle with the guardrail.

There, choking and coughing on stale air bag dust, Norton and Chub made for what the TV news described as, "A fifty-car pile up and the largest traffic jam in the history of Interstate 35."

In their defense, the pile-up was more of a massive bumper-to-bumper and the news reports blew everything out of proportion. Sure, people were stuck in traffic for hours and the school was reduced to rubble, but you should know that, miraculously, the only casualties were the three cows Norton ran over while crossing the pasture.

Norton and Chub flashed across national headlines. "Elderly men charged with arson," read one, "Ice Cream Kills Cows," read another—each headline accompanied by mug shots of the men covered in ice cream.

The only human injury resulting from this chain reaction was a bruise on the side of someone's head, that someone's head being Chub's. The doctor felt sympathetic and told the nurses that,

due to Chub's concussion, Chub could eat all the hambone soup he

so pleased. The nurses, however, having children that went to

Folkston Elementary, held him in quite a bit of disregard.

Chub's hospital visit was far from pleasant. He was used

to having Norton around, rather than an unfriendly police officer

named Ty. The officer was present due to the potential danger that

Chub posed, but he could see Chub was harmless, and Ty was just

there to satisfy protocol. Norton, meanwhile, was waiting for the

court hearing down at the local jail; the same place Chub would

meet him after his recovery.

*****

Norton and Chub tried to act as though they weren't looking when the man sat down. His face tightened upon making contact with the seat. Norton assumed this was due to the coldness. Chub wondered how someone could expect him to use the barbarous contraption. There were no doors to guard one from prying eyes. *Such a vulnerable position,* he thought.

The man leaned over now, unfurling a roll of toilet paper. This is when they were approached by a different fellow, one who had been fashioning a styrofoam cup in the corner.

"You see this?" The fellow asked, holding the cup upward.

"This is how you make an air filter." He tilted the cup so they could see the bottom had been cut out. Norton and Chub watched as he stood on their bench and stuck the cup onto a paper clip that was hanging from a vent over head. Reaching into his

pocket he pulled out a roll of toothpaste and applied a generous

amount to the interior of the cup. By the time he stepped down, the

smell of mint leaves had entered their noses. This was much more

pleasant than the smell of a poo-stained toilet.

"Jail tricks," said the fellow. "You'll learn all of them if

you're in here long enough."

Chub thought about that for a moment. He hoped he

wouldn't learn all of them. He was far from fond of the place. The

seats were hard and the lights were harsh. Chub began to compare

and contrast his experience with what he had seen of jail on TV.

Another man was now sitting on the toilet reading the newspaper.

Chub felt struck by the offhand manner in which he whistled *Don't*

Worry, Be Happy with his pants atop his ankles.

From the opposing cell, a responding whistle came

through the wall. Norton picked up on it immediately. *"The Fishin'*

Hole whistle," he said.

"From the *Andy Griffith Show*!" said Chub.

What followed was an exchange of upbeat whistled tunes

between the two cells. This went on while Norton persisted in

trying to teach a stranger how to juggle with two nickels and a

dime.

"Hey," came a loud voice from outside the cell,

accompanied by a loud knock on the doors window. A guard stood

outside, shaking his nightstick. "You're not supposed to have

those," he said, entering the room to take the pocket change away

from Norton.

"Matter of fact," said the guard, his head pointed at

Norton and Chub. "Why don't you two come sit outside with me?

Your case starts in ten minutes, anyway."

CHAPTER FOUR

The judge was old. The judge was mean. The judge was

not a friend.

She smacked slowly and wide and Chub disliked the

pink blob tumbling around her teeth. "Gum's not supposed to do

that . . ." he thought, watching the judge push it through one of the

crooked gaps. Chub was unsure if the creature behind the podium

was human. She bore a face that never changed. Her lips were

lined straight and her eyes un-turning, changing direction only when she moved her head. She seemed lifeless, lifeless in the sense that she were simply a body, hollowed out with no core or insides, no heart or gut to feel right or wrong—no mind to judge or evaluate the difference.

"The decision has been made," said the judge, in the only way she knew how. Harshly.

Norton spoke up, "But—".

"But nothing," said the judge. "When the jury hears the testimony of the children. . ." she belched, "Oh! The children!" Quickly, she relaxed her posture and straightened out her gown by pulling it down, apparently collecting herself from a clear break in character. "They will feel as I do."

After resuming her lifeless pose, she continued speaking, "When they hear the testimony of the children. . . they will agree with my decision. The two men before us are a hazard to society, they cannot and should not be left to their own devices."

Chub cringed when the judge let out another screech, "All rise!".

Everyone in the courtroom began to move, their wooden chairs sliding against the grain of the floors. Perking up, and onto their feet, Norton and Chub stood in attention.

"We have been gathered here today. . ." the judge started out, giving the standard opening she had been giving for years. For Norton and Chub, the words slowly faded off into the uneasy stillness of the room. They did not feel as if they were listening to a trial, but rather to a eulogy.

After telling everyone to be seated, the judge lifted her chin and gazed distantly into the room, "Taking to the stand is our first witness, *little Susie,"* she then softened her voice, "Sweetie, if

you wouldn't mind, now is the time for you to come up here just

like we rehearsed okay?"

All Norton could think was, *Rehearsed. . . rehearsed?*

They rehearsed this!

Each head pivoted to the sound of soft clacks originating

in the back of the room as the red shoes on Susie's feet began to

prance forward. All Norton and Chub could see were the tops of

golden French braids bobbing across the aisle. On a different

occasion, in a room like this, she would have been an innocent

flower girl. The jury, after all, did see her as innocent. With the

books they had to sit on her seat in order to give her a boost, it was

hard not to. Little Susie could hardly see over the witness stand.

Child after child took to the stand and spoke with pre-scripted remarks, most likely given to them by the school board. Norton and Chub found sitting patiently to be hard. The grievances of the children were clearly an act. The two men couldn't help but feel as if they were getting served. One boy apparently forgot his script at home and, to the dismay of his parents and the tune of a grin, said he was just happy he didn't have to go to school. A chuckle broke out in the room. Norton snuck a complementary high-five while the boy was on the way back to his seat. Yet the truthful boy's testimony was not enough. After the jury reconvened, the sentence was dealt.

"Having been found guilty of the charges against you, brought forth by the state, this court hereby sentences you to Dave Springs Nursing Home."

"A nursing home!" yelled Norton. "Chub and I can take care of ourselves just fine."

"Apparently not," said the judge. "I see no other way to settle this. The city of Phoenix has been receiving complaints about your ice cream truck for a year now and seeing as how you two have no money to settle the lawsuits, the jury and I have been left with no other option. The home recently celebrated its one-hundredth anniversary and has a long history. There are a lot of your. . . your, um. . . your types there." She smiled for the first time since the proceeding started, "You will be in good hands. And believe me. You two got *lucky*. There are much worse places we could have sent you than Dave Springs."

*****

"Where are they taking us?" Norton complained. He was looking out his window at a vast desert expanse and wiping sweat off his forehead.

"We have your stupid cigarettes to blame," said Chub, his arms crossed. "I knew those things would come back to get you. I didn't know they would come back to get me too!"

They were riding in a white prison bus, heading down a bumpy dirt road. The driver seemed not to mind the bumps too much, nor the complaints of his passengers.

"The wheels are going to fall off this thing," Norton spoke up, but instead of responding, the driver simply reached down and turned the radio up a little louder.

Sitting atop the springy driver's seat and bouncing

around, the boy wore a frayed cowboy hat and a cut off T-shirt. He

was a young kid, probably just out of high-school, and perhaps a

little too caught up in the song playing on the radio. Norton

couldn't figure out if the kid really thought he could sing, or if he

just enjoyed tormenting his passengers.

> *After two days in the desert sun*
> *My skin began to turn red*
>
> *After three days in the desert fun*
>
> *I was looking at a river bed*
>
> *And the story it told of a river that flowed*
>
> *Made me sad to think it was dead*

"Oh please," said Norton loudly, realizing what the boy

was trying to do. But the enchantment worked on Chub, as he

found himself in a trance-like state, dwelling on the desert sun and

the strange place they were in.

You see I've been through the desert on a horse

with no name

It felt good to be out of the rain

Suddenly the radio cut out and a frizzy noise came over the

speakers. "Ah, come on," said the boy. He rapped on the radio with

the bottom of his fist, heard frizz, then rapped on it a few times

more.

In the desert you can remember your name

'Cause there ain't no one for to give you no

pain

La, la, la la la la, la la la, la la...

Other than Norton, Chub, and the driver there was only one other person on the bus. She leaned over towards Chub with a picture in her hand, "This is my grandson," she said, her eyes beaming.

The woman held out the picture a little longer than either Norton or Chub cared to look at it, but the whole time they smiled and acted as if they were interested nonetheless. "I wonder about him everyday," she said. "He does well in school."

The boy in the picture was a bit plump and had pink cheeks.

"Looks like Chub when he was younger," said Norton.

Chub silently took offense as the woman placed the picture back in her purse.

"Say, why exactly are you heading to the nursing home? If you don't mind my asking." Norton looked genuinely curious.

"Oh, me?" she blushed, and then chuckled, "I stabbed my husband."

Norton and Chub grew wide eyes. They sat up straighter and looked out their window, as if what they just heard was never said or didn't register. The elderly woman came off as a little too feeble, a little too sweet. The three then sat there in their own minds, thinking of things they could say to keep the conversation going. Nothing seemed right.

Directly ahead, a building could be seen far off on the simmering horizon. As they got closer, Norton made out a large sign hanging above the front doors.

'Welcome to Dave Springs Nursing Home', the sign said, or was supposed to say. The sign lacked even the slightest semblance of professionalism. The words *'Welcome to Dave Springs'* were written large, and the words *'Nursing Home'* got progressively smaller. Norton figured whoever painted the sign must have noticed they were running out of room, and, in an attempt to make everything fit on the board, began painting smaller and smaller letters.

"What kind of a nursing home is this?" Norton asked the driver. He was now examining the rusty fence that stretched around the compound.

"Ha!" barked the driver. "This is no nursing home. . ."

"Then what is it," Norton asked? "And why does it say 'Dave Springs Nursing Home' above the door if it's not a nursing home?"

"That's a good question," said the driver. "All I know is no one here ever gets any visitors. No one ever takes this bus out either. They only take it in. And I don't know about you, but I've never seen no nursing home with a barbed wire fence befores."

Chub rubbed his eyes real good, then opened them and squinted back at the home. He was really craving a Choco Taco right about now.

CHAPTER FIVE

When the three passengers stepped off the bus they were pleasantly greeted by a short man, the most notable of his features being the circular glasses and handlebar mustache. Together with his black suspenders and grey bow tie, the look came together well.

"Hey! I'm Otto," the man said, "I've been tasked with helping you guys get through processing. After that, if you want, I'll be happy to give you a tour of the grounds."

Otto was a skinny yet energetic fellow. That he was happy provided a glimmer of hope for the two. The little man had a gleeful aurora about him. *Maybe the home will be nice on the inside,* Norton and Chub thought to themselves, their attitudes hopeful.

"If you think it looks like a strange place" Otto began, "then you would right. Before it became a nursing home, the government called it Lair Nine. At the time of construction, it was the largest missile silo in the world. Some secret squirrel shit."

Otto shook his head in what appeared to be a disturbed manner, "Now that I think of it," he said, "it still is some secret squirrel shit." He paused but only briefly, "Anyways, never mind that. We'll talk about it when the time comes. Here's all you need to know. Four great corridors run diagonally and converge at a center point, making the nursing home look like a giant X from the sky."

Missile silo? Norton kept thinking. *Missile silo?* He wanted to slow Otto down but he didn't have the chance. Otto was speaking fast, clearly excited to welcome his guests.

"There is a perimeter fence that surrounds this parking lot in the front and a cemetery at the back, while on either side of this X in the open spaces between, a courtyard exists for the pleasure of its residents. One side of the X we call Wing A, or the Wardens side, and the other side we call Wing B. You will be staying in Wing B."

A moment passed and Otto finally gave them a chance to let things sink in.

"I hope you brought sunscreen," said Otto, scanning at the top of Norton's nearly bald head. "They don't provide that in here. Of course, you won't need sunscreen if you never go outside, some residents rarely do, but, that's when you slowly start to decline, if you know what I mean?"

Norton looked over at Otto out of the corner of his eye.

"I know how to make sunscreen," said Otto, his tone coming off a bit too chipper. "If you ever need any, I have a herbal remedy. Came up with it myself. Would probably make good money off it if I wasn't stuck in here."

Otto looked at the large suitcase the woman wheeled behind her, and then down at the duffle bags Norton and Chub were dragging through the dirt, "You guys brought more than most people do. I've seen some walk in with nothing but the clothes on their back." He paused for a moment. "Say, you three wouldn't happen to have a lint roller would you? I've been meaning to get my hands on one."

Norton and Chub glanced over at each other thinking that was an odd thing to ask. Looking wryly at Otto, they shook their heads. Chub noticed the nicely pressed lines running down Otto's sleeves. *He seems like the type of person to care about lint*, Chub thought before feeling slightly embarrassed by the fact that Otto's shirt was spotless and his own bore an easily noticeable stain.

"I have a roller," said the woman.

"Well then," said Otto, "How would you like two bottles of my special sunscreen in exchange?"

"Sounds like a fine deal to me," said the woman, "I've already got a few sun spots, wouldn't want them to get any worse."

"You two look like brothers," Otto was looking them over.

"We are" said Chub.

"Almost didn't notice."

Norton was wearing a hawaiian t-shirt and a pair of khaki jeans with nice brown dress shoes. Otto thought he looked rather dapper for a man of his age. Chub, meanwhile, wore a pair of suspenders like Otto, only his suspenders were red and a bit more worn out than Otto's. He had a belly that hung below his belt, shorts that were hiked up six-inches above the knee, and a pair of white socks that ran up moderately hairy legs. In Otto's mind he was a carbon-cut copy of what a Dave Springs resident should look like. *A wonder*, he thought, *that the two brothers would dress so differently.*

After Otto had finished escorting the three through processing, they began making their way out to the courtyard but were stopped by a raspy voice coming out of a nearby room. "Oh please, bring them in here," the voice said.

Otto stopped and closed his eyes. Norton could tell something about this gesture indicated he did not want to enter the room.

When they rounded the corner Otto said, "This is Grumpy, she has been here for... five, ten, what is it, fifteen lifetimes now?"

Grumpy pursed her lips then said, "Oh hush Otto, how rude of you to introduce me that way." She lifted her chin, "My name is Susana Ogletree. That is what I prefer to go by. I have Otto to thank for the name Grumpy. Everyone calls me that now. All he does is run around here playing jokes and nicknaming people. A lousy way to pass time if you ask me. Lord knows he needs the good book. Probably doesn't even have one."

"What's that you're crocheting," said the woman who was on the bus with Norton and Chub.

"Oh this, this will be a coaster when I am through. They ought to look nice on my dining table. You like to crochet?"

"I find it splendid," said the woman perking up.

"Why don't you join me? You don't really want to spend the rest of your day walking around with Otto and—" Grumpy looked Chub up and down, "that thing do you?"

Chub turned around to see if anybody was standing behind him.

"Oh!" The woman said, "But Otto has been nice and..." she looked at Chub, "he's been swell too. Besides, Otto was about to give us a tour of the courtyard and show us our rooms."

"Listen here, um, I'm sorry, what is your name?" Grumpy asked.

"Martha"

"Listen here Martha, I've got a wide collection of spools from which you can crochet and we've all day to show you your room. Set your things down right there. You know what they say, 'hang around dogs and you'll pick up fleas.' We wouldn't want that now would we?"

"Dogs?" Norton laughed at the audacity of the woman, "Ha! You just met us and we've yet to speak a word. What makes you think we're dogs?"

"I know a dog when I see one," said Grumpy, she then looked over at Martha, "Listen girl, that sunscreen you got off

Otto, you see it? Well… it'll turn your skin green. And it itches. He tries that trick on everyone." Grumpy let out an evil sigh "You don't want to hang around Otto for too long okay? He'll ruin your reputation. Very few of the women like Otto."

"Hey Otto!", said a woman passing by in the hallway. "Hey Mrs. Olson," Otto responded cheerfully, "Thanks for the peanut butter cookies!"

Grumpy frowned. "Pick your team," she said sternly.

Martha glanced down at her sunscreen, angry that she had been duped, "I guess I'll stay here with you."

"All right then, without further adieu, we three dogs shall make our way to the courtyard." Otto bowed with an air of suave, "Martha, I hope you enjoy your stay." He then turned to Grumpy and said, "As you were."

On their way out the room, Norton looked over at Chub. Both Norton and Chub were thinking the same thing. The green sunscreen was a clever trick, but neither of them would have wanted to pull it on Martha, not after what she told them on the bus. She was, after all, in the home for murder.

A few paces up the hall and Otto was opening the door to a tiled room. A heavy muskiness hit their noses as Norton and Chub laid eyes on the squeamish green walls. Throughout the room, silver spigots were protruding from the tiles, beneath each of which a long rust stain ran down the wall to the floor. These stains ultimately met in the center of the room at a circular drain. Norton noticed the drain lacked a cover. He made a mental note not to step in it when he got a shower. Chub, however, was busy trying to think of ways to avoid the shower all together. *So repulsive,* he thought, *no curtains, slimy soap bars all over the floor. God knows what else.*

"By the way, I advise you always shower with someone else," said Otto. "Frankie and Gomez have been known to… er, get close we'll say."

"This Frankie and Gomez, what do they look like?" Norton asked.

"You should be able to figure it out. They're the only men in the home who dress like Grumpy and Martha." Otto wound up the hall and turned to a door that had the number 33 on it. "Norton, this is the room you have been assigned, and Chub, this room here," he pointed at the adjacent door, "is the room you have been assigned." He handed over two pairs of keys, "I'll let you guys have the honors."

Norton took the key. The lock could be heard moving within the mechanism. Chub decided to walk in behind him.

"You'll notice," said Otto, "That most of the other residents have a couch. If you want one you'll have to request it at the time of someone's passing."

"We have to wait until someone dies to get a couch?"

"Yes, but don't worry, you shouldn't have to wait long."

Chub thought he might be losing his mind.

Norton looked in the bedroom to see a concaved mattress on a ragged frame. "So... who was the last person to croak in it?"

"Old Man Parkins," said Otto, the dimples formed by his smile pointing up towards his ears like arrows. "Welcome to the home."

They walked out to tour Chub's room, which looked exactly the same, except for the pink stain on the bedroom floor that could have passed for either throw up or blood.

"Let's head to the courtyard," said Otto, fixated on the stain with Norton and Chub, his voice queasy.

Once out in the sun the three could hear a loud ruckus. By all appearances, there seemed to be some sort of mob gathering in the furthest corner of the yard. People could be heard cheering and booing and yelling all sorts of things. "You're going to get killed", a woman screeched, followed by a, "What are you doing with that thing?"

Norton and Chub were on edge, their minds running over what kind of madness could be unfolding. Otto looked down at the timepiece he was slowly pulling out of his pocket, then casually began walking towards the crowd to see for himself.

"The man you are about to behold is Choctaw," said Otto. The three were pushing through to the center of the crowd. When they got there, they saw a man who stood about six foot four, a series of bones beaded around his neck.

"And now," said Choctaw to the crowd, "I shall release the snake from the bag, just to show you that I can catch him again."

The tall figure was walking around the circle that had formed, stretching a brown bag outward so that everyone could see it, the face of each spectator that of awe.

Choctaw released the bag into the middle of the circle. After some prodding with his staff, a rattlesnake slipped out and onto the sand. The snake hissed and poised itself tensely for attack; it's rattle making its intentions known.

Choctaw began chanting and twisting back and forth before the snake. A belt with colorful feathers bounced around his waist. Choctaw courted the snake, and then picked him up with his staff, taunting the crowd, jeering and making everyone back up. Then, dropping the snake, Choctaw stamped its head into the ground with his cowboy boot. Pulling out a vial from his chest pocket, Choctaw reached down with his other hand

and grabbed the snake just behind the head, showing his spectators the fangs.

"This is the Mohave Rattlesnake," said Choctaw, presenting it before the crowd. "She can grow up to 5 feet long. One of the longest we have here in Arizona." He raised the vial in his other hand. "I will now show you how to milk a snake of it's venom." A few of the men in the crowd had gaping jaws, almost all of the women had either a hand over their mouth or were peaking through their fingers. "Just four ounces of venom from this snake can fetch a man eight hundred dollars." He was carefully bringing the vial up towards the snake's fangs. "You see, she is, by some experts, considered the most toxic rattlesnake in the—ARGH!" One of the fangs missed the cloth lining on the vial. "AH! Ah uh..." Choctaws face went white and he started pacing. "Um, it's okay, everyone. This, as you'll see, is part of the—Argh," he pulled the fang out of his hand, "show."

"Everyone carry on now," he said, "Know that I will be okay. I have been trained by my elders. I know how to treat these things. Thankfully, this was only one fang. But let this be a lesson, even a master snake handler can be bit."

The whole crowd began to clap their hands. A man from the back yelled, "Do it again!"

*****

Later that evening, Norton and Chub spent time helping Otto take care of Choctaw. He was reclined back on his couch with his hand propped on the armrest. Outside the window the sky was beginning to turn pink and Otto had just got back from the ice machine with another bag of ice. He laid it gently over Choctaws right arm.

"The importance is to keep calm," said Choctaw.

Chub's eyes were wide open and had been since Choctaw got bit. "I will be okay." Choctaw said while looking at Chub, "You on the other hand, I am not sure about." He looked concerned, "Otto, go fetch this man a snickers from my fridge, and maybe a Coca-Cola. Get one for yourself and Norton while you're at it."

Otto disappeared into the kitchen and then brought the treats back into the living room.

"Lads, you two are obviously new around here?"

Norton looked up at Choctaw, "Unfortunately...."

"Hmm... you should know some things then." Choctaw started to move his arm and straighten up on the couch but an agonizing pain shot up his shoulder and he remembered his impairment. "Argh—Anyways... I was going to say that Otto is the man who can get whatever you need. That is one of the things he is known for. People go to him and request all sorts of stuff. He never disappoints. How he does it I do not know. Be it a box of cigars or a fine bottle of wine, Otto is your man. Stay in good company with Otto and stay away from the Warden. Do those two things and you'll—" Choctaw stopped, "I guess there's three things. You should also stay away from Frankie and Gomez."

Otto then returned to the room without Norton and Chub having realized he left. This time, instead of walking back with Cokes and Sneaker bars, he was carrying three sleeping bags. Otto unfurled them long-ways, their zippers undone and stretched out on the floor like quilts. "Too hot to get in them," he said, "we'll lay on-top."

Norton was thinking of Old Man Parkins, the man who died in the very bed he was supposed to sleep in. Chub, meanwhile, was thinking of the nasty stain on his bedroom floor. For their first nights stay, both of them were happy to sleep in Choctaws room.

"I want to keep an eye on him," said Otto, "that snake bite has me worried."

Choctaw grinned and said he was fine, but Otto could tell he would enjoy the company too.

CHAPTER SIX

Otto couldn't help but watch as Norton's head bobbed up and down. And then up. And then down. After a pitiful attempt to raise his head once more, the chin above Norton's shoulders succumbed to gravity and slowly rested itself upon his chest.

"He fell asleep in the back of a taxi cab once. Woke up three hours and eighty dollars later," said Chub. "Another time he passed out and put a dent in our mailbox."

The three were sitting down in the cafeteria.

"Does he have narcolepsy?" Otto asked.

"Narcolepsy...?"

Chub was uncertain what the word meant. Otto grabbed Norton and, after a good shake, Norton's head slowly started to rise. "Wake up buddy. I'm trying to point out people, give you their names." Otto waited for Norton to regain consciousness. "That over there," Norton and Chub turned to look in the direction Otto was pointing. A man stood by the windows rocking back and forth. "That is Fran. All Fran tells anybody is, "'I'm Fran. I've been certified for 53 years, 2 months, 3 days, and...' you get the idea."

"This is Arm Pitt," said Otto, "Arm Pitt, this is Norton and Chub."

Arm Pitt bent down to sit at the table, a tin spit cup which he had attached to his belt clanked on the seat. "Hey guys," he said, his tone somewhere between casual enthusiasm and indifference.

"When Arm Pitt moved in they had to take the ceiling fan out of his room. That mark on his forehead is from one of the blades. He's tall and big and sweats half his weight a day. Probably doesn't help he no longer has a ceiling fan. Arm Pitts nickname caught on exceptionally fast. Perhaps due to everyone being under the impression I was, that if we called him Arm Pitt he might actually start using deodorant."

Arm Pitt spoke up protesting.

"It's true," said Otto. "He still forgets deodorant. But anyways, as I was saying, Arm Pitt was thrown into Dave Springs after shooting a game warden in the thigh, weren't you Arm Pitt?"

"Yep. Got em good."

"Arm Pitt tried to claim he thought the warden was a deer, but it wasn't even deer season, was it Arm Pitt?"

"Nope. Should have said he looked like a turkey."

"Surprisingly, the Judge was only going to charge him with a reasonable fine. This was not enough for the game warden, though. Two weeks after the trial a full-on investigation was launched and the ATF wound up on his doorstep. In his possession were ten live hand grenades, five sticks of dynamite, two tons of gunpowder and nine illegal firearms. One of which he used to shoot the warden."

"They found my moonshine still too. Searched my property over good. There's a few things they didn't find though." Arm Pitt smiled then shoveled a spoonful of porridge into his mouth. "Hey—" he swallowed his food and asked, "you guys starting in the cabbage patch today?"

"Cabbage patch?" Chub asked.

"Otto hasn't told you about it yet?"

Norton scratched his head and Arm Pitt could tell he was distracted by something. "Who is that?" Norton asked. He was staring at a man wearing a veteran's cap with a Purple Heart clipped to the brim.

Otto looked over his right shoulder, then over his left, inching closer to Norton's ear. "That's Badger. He always sits at the end of the table, keeping one seat between himself and Arm Pitt. My advice is that you don't ask Badger about his Purple Heart. Badger doesn't like to talk about the war. The man spent eighty days in the tunnels. Eighty solid days. When he finally crawled out, following closely behind him were three American prisoners. He was a hero. And I probably shouldn't tell you this, but..." he leaned further into Norton, "Badger has a little wooden box in his room with twenty seven thumbs in it. He also has a scroll of parchment upon which he mapped nearly twelve miles of uncharted tunnels. When Badger talks, people listen."

A lump rolled down Norton's throat. He did not know where he was, but he did know it was a place he did not like. Sitting there he began to look around the cafeteria. Most of the residents sat soundlessly as they ate their food. The brick walls were an aged white, painted sometime ago, now yellow. "There is this presence about the place," Norton told Otto, "a smell of something. I don't like it."

"When I moved in I had to take the batteries out of my watch," said Otto, "Every second it would slap the silence. I hated it. The thing just kept ticking and I had no TV or radio or anything to tone it out." Otto stopped for a moment, "I guess what I'm trying to say is I know what you mean. You try not to think about it. Occupy your mind with other things."

"Oh! Ouch," said Chub. His eyes were fixed on Choctaw's right arm, now a fine shade of blue and swollen to the size of a pineapple. Choctaw had just sat down at the table.

"Baha!" Badger broke out, "We'll start calling him Pop-Eye now. How do you like that nickname Otto?"

Otto simply shook his head.

"Once an Indian now a sailorman!" Badger laughed. Arm Pitt followed him up with a good-ol-boy chuckle, "Ah-huh-huh."

"Yeah haha, jokes on me," said Choctaw with a bit of disdain.

"We've already given him a nickname Badger. He is Choctaw. There is no need for another. We should all just be glad he is okay."

Badger continued to wheeze on his joke.

"You guys starting in the cabbage patch today," Choctaw asked?

"Arm Pit asked that a few seconds ago, before you sat down."

"Oh."

"Yes," said Otto, "They'll be starting after lunch. Has the Warden ever given anyone their second day off?"

"He gave me off," said Arm Pit.

"Probably forgot to tell you that you needed to be working."

"Work," Norton asked?

"All able bodied residents are required to—"

"What?" Norton asked again, this time much louder. "They can't force us to work!"

"Well," Arm Pitt began, "some people enjoy it. The ladies in particular, but... for me, having done some gardening back home, it's kind of nice."

"The cabbage patch," said Badger, "ain't no garden and it ain't no patch. It's part farm, part factory, the kind where there's always work to do. No fun for me. I see it for what it is."

"I didn't see no farm coming in," Chub said.

"Everything in time," said Otto, "And Badger, you know it's not that bad." Otto changed the subject. "You guys like Bingo?" Otto looked to Chub and then to Norton.

Norton piped up sarcastically, "You mean that boring game only old people play? Please tell me that's not all I have to look forward to in here."

"Only ten bucks for a card."

Norton spoke again, "You lose more than you win with those types of things. Research proves it."

"I never lose," said Otto smiling, "I am the home's leprechaun."

Arm Pitt set down a toothpick he was using and said, "He's not lying. Rarely plays, but when he does..."

"I don't know how he does it," said Badger.

"I never get lucky," Chub frowned.

"Ah, it's all just fun and games," said Otto, "Gives everyone something to look forward to. I tell you what Chub, sometime today I'll be sure to teach you my bingo strategy."

"Bingo strategy?" asked Norton. "You can't be serious. How could anyone possibly have a *Bingo strategy*?"

"I don't know," said Arm Pitt, "but he's certainly got something."

Otto stood up to go dump his tray and Norton and Chub rose to follow.

Once out in the hallway the three strolled down the corridor of Wing B. Otto told Norton and Chub about the type of work they would do in the cabbage patch. He ran over the typical tasks one might expect to do in a garden; things like water the plants, till the soil, plant seeds and fertilize.

"Oh, and everything's underground," said Otto, finishing his train of thought.

"Underground?" Norton asked, a puzzled look on his face.

"I told you. Dave Springs is an old missile silo, remember?"

CHAPTER SEVEN

The elevator gave a lurch and began moving down the shaft. A concrete wall passed on the other side of the glass doors and floor one came into view. *Ding!,* came an echo around the small compartment. The doors slid open and Martha walked out with Grumpy into a field of green.

"Dominican Haze," said Otto.

Odd name, Norton thought, *must be some sort of spice.*

The elevator lurched again. A concrete floor passed and Norton noticed the red number above the clear doors change to a two. He and Chub were suddenly staring at another field of green, albeit this field seemed a lighter shade.

"Devil's Blue," said Otto.

The doors slid open and Choctaw walked in. "What floor you guys headed to?"

"We're going down to floor forty eight," said Otto.

"Forty eight?" Norton asked, shocked by the revelation, now noticing the button for number 48 was lit up.

"I'm on ten," said Choctaw, "they've got me rolling today."

"These plants..." Norton started, catching a whiff of something familiar, "they're not what I think they are?" The smell always accompanied the Winslow boys and their low-rider. It was especially pungent the day they threw the egg at his mailbox.

"What... ganga? Herb?" Choctaw chortled, "I guess there might be a little of that down here. Just a little."

Above the doors the number now read three.

"Uptown Raw," said Otto, continuing to call out the name of each passing strain, floor by floor. "Chernobyl Bionic... Grape Ape... Ninja Purp... Sour Diesel... Northern Lights... Maui Wowie... G13... Blueberry Bud... White Widow... Columbian

Dark... Aussie Blues... Pomegranate Kush... Afghani Delight... Albino Rhino... Elephant Bud... Laughing Grass... Donkey Nut..."

When the elevator finally made it down to floor forty-eight, a small plume of dust rolled up from under the doors. Otto lead them into a closet lined with white jumpsuits. Chub felt his ears pop as Otto instructed the two on the best way to climb in. "I don't wear my shoes," he said, shaking the white booty attached to the bottom of the suit. Soon they were geared up and, staring through black veils on their hoodies, Otto guided Norton and Fudge out of the closet and into a different room.

"This is where we mix the fertilizer," he said, pointing at two large containers. One contained a fine blue powder and the other a silvery liquid. After using a vacuum hose to transfer the powder into the silvery substance, Otto donned a large backpack tank.

"Fill me up," he said, looking over to Norton. "You can use the same vacuum hose."

The humdrum of a vacuum filled the room again. Within several moments the three were each standing with fertilizer tanks on their backs. This growing room was just like the others, only instead of containing long rectangular troughs filled with plants, it contained long rectangular troughs filled with nothing but soil.

"Norton, you'll get this side and Chub can get the other. I'll work on the row beside you incase you need anything. Pretty easy job, just spray and walk."

The room stretched out nearly as far as one could see. Neither Norton nor Chub could believe how long it took to traverse the entire length. Norton rocked his body forward, slinging the fertilizer tank higher on his back. Chub watched as Norton attempted to readjust the weight displacement. Fertilizer sloshed around as he tightened down his straps. Their shoulder muscles were flattened and deprived of blood. Otto assured them that their packs would get lighter as they used more fertilizer.

Sweat began to sting at Otto's eyes, pooling into the tips of his gloves and beading up at the hairline on the back of his neck. He knew that Norton and Chub must be sweating too. The suits, while meant to keep toxic fertilizer out, doubled to keep perspiration in.

"The good news is we only have this floor to fertilize," said Otto. "Tomorrow we'll probably be up on floor one, or maybe floor ten. Floor ten is processing."

Norton was glad to hear he wouldn't have to smell the fertilizer anymore. Every hair in his nose felt as though it were curling up and beginning to singe. The smell was astringent, actively corroding and breaking down the air, along with everything in it.

"What is this stuff made of?" Norton asked.

"I don't know. Got some in my mouth one day, tasted like some sort of sour mix between ammonia and ethanol."

Chub looked down at Norton's side. There was a tear in his suit. Chub noticed the pale roundness of Norton's belly, then the swath of chafed red skin. Norton dug his thumb beneath the side strap on his backpack and tried to pry it outward. He felt wetness and assumed it was sweat. Chub saw that it was blood. The pack had been cutting into Norton's side.

Alerting him of the wound, Norton simply chocked it up to old age. "Had alligator skin in the young days," he said, thinking of how his body looked now, scattered with sun spots and bruises from ruptured veins.

The three pressed on in silence, each humoring their own thoughts, Chub thinking of food, Otto preoccupied by the next Bingo game, Norton mesmerized by the immensity of the cabbage patch.

Like this they carried on until finally, after a monotonous eight hours, the three were climbing back into the elevator shaft and heading up to the surface at last.

*****

Upon exiting the elevator, Otto lead Norton and Chub down the hall. Three women were sitting at one of the lobby tables. Otto decided to approach them. "Ladies, how do we do?" he asked.

Grumpy and Martha glanced up at the men, then at one another, and then back down at the puzzle they had been working on, a perturbed look on their faces.

"We're doing okay, I guess…" said the third woman after a moment of silence turned into two.

"Norton, Chub… this is Hagrith. Hagrith, this is—"

"I know who they are," said Hagrith sternly.

Otto noticed Chub acting a little squeamish. He seemed as though he were trying to suppress a giggle. Otto decided not to think much of it. Instead, he was trying to figure out the lies Grumpy must have been pouring into Martha's head. Undoubtedly, Grumpy had been trying to make Martha hate Otto as much as she did.

"That's a lot of puzzle pieces."

"Thirty two thousand," said Hagrith.

"What do you care Otto," said Grumpy.

"Oh I don't really. Puzzle's have never been my thing. I've just never seen one that big."

"We're going to get it framed when we finish it," said Hagrith, who was apparently under the impression that assembling the puzzle would be some sort of philanthropic achievement.

Otto looked down at the picture on the puzzle box.

"A unicorn?" he asked. "You don't think a red barn, or a waterfall or an old white house would be more appropriate? Stained walls seem preferable to me over a unicorn."

"Then why don't you do that," said Grumpy. "If you want a waterfall hung on the wall, you can put your own puzzle together."

"I'd just buy a poster," said Otto, turning to leave.

When they got further down the hallway Chub let go of the giggle he had been suppressing.

"What are you on about?" Otto asked.

"We have a pocket full of pieces," said Norton, "I think one of the pieces is the unicorn's eyeball. A few of the others might be one of its ears."

"I knew there was a reason I liked you guys," said Otto, "I'll show you two what your room can look like." With that the three men soon found themselves crossing the hall to Otto's room. As Norton and Chub walked in they studied all the trinkets scattered around. A round vacuum cleaner robot was gliding around on the floor, first bouncing off his couch and then off his coffee table. "What is this," Chub asked. He was looking into a glass display case.

Otto opened the case and handed a Megalodon shark tooth to Chub so he could hold it. "I found it while diving the Cooper River in South Carolina." Before passing the tooth to Norton, Chub rubbed his forefinger across the tooths jagged edge to see how sharp it was.

"I actually found the arrow heads out in the courtyard. Choctaw could tell you more about them than I can. He said this one here is a Clovis point, possibly ten thousand years old."

Norton and Chub could tell Otto was proud of his artifact collection. "Have a seat," he said. "Chub, I'm about to show you how I play Bingo." Reaching over he grabbed his laptop and a Bingo card off the coffee table. Norton and Chub watched as Otto pulled up a picture of the number sixteen on his laptop. "These numbers have already been called," he said, running his finger down the row that ran along the right side of the card. "All I need is that last one, number sixteen." He pulled a pingpong ball out of his pants pocket. "This will be number sixteen." A printer in the corner of the room suddenly came to life and shot out a glossy piece of paper with a small number sixteen on it.

"I don't get it," said Norton. "Adding a ball with the number sixteen on it doesn't really increase your odds that much."

Otto held a persistent smile as he got up and went to the printer. Norton and Chub watched as Otto gingerly transferred the fresh ink onto the ping pong ball. He then went to a cabinet in the kitchen and drew out a syringe. "This is a 40 gauge needle," he said, "Very small. So small in fact, that the olive oil I am about to inject into the ball will not be able to leak out. The oil is too thick to seep back through. When the warden turns the wheel tomorrow, being the heaviest ball in the mix, ball number sixteen will sink to the bottom, right where I need it to be. A little door will open, and my money will roll out right into the Warden's hand." Otto pressed the needle into the ball and injected some of the oil. "It takes about half an ounce," he said, "thirteen grams to be precise."

"I feel the urge to applaud you," said Norton, "How much do you think you'll win?"

"It's been several weeks since the last time someone won. I know it's over two hundred bucks. I don't know the exact number, though."

Chub thought about all the things he could buy with two hundred dollars.

"Who is the Warden?" Norton asked, scratching his head. "I'd imagine a lot of people would be upset if they found out you were doing this."

"The warden is the man who runs Dave Springs. And yes, sometimes I do feel guilty about it," said Otto, "but I only cheat about three times a year, and I intentionally lose a few cards here and there, just so people don't get suspicious. It's not like I don't put anything in at all. Besides, the warden steals more than I do anyway. He pockets half of the money that goes into the pot. So while we residents may put in five hundred, we only stand a chance at winning two hundred. Crummy deal if you ask me. I would start a boycott over it if it wasn't so easy for me to win every now and then."

"The people here have nothing to say about the warden pocketing that much?"

"They complain about it all the time but they still play the stupid game," Otto wavered for a second, "Speaking of the warden... it's in your best interest he doesn't get to know you." Otto let out a deep sigh. "There used to be a guy around here named Arnold Selinski. He got along with everyone, as down to earth as anyone could be. Not long after he moved in he was caught sneaking around the premises. Went missing and no one knew where to. Some thought he was shipped off somewhere else, others thought the warden killed him. One month passed, then two, then three. Finally four months later we saw him in the lunch line again. That guy I pointed out to you that was standing by the windows earlier? The one that was rocking back and forth? That guy used to be Arnold Selinski. The warden locked him in a dark room and played the same recording over and over again, 'I'm Fran. I've been certified for 53 years, 2 months, 9 days, and 6 hours.'

I made an attempt to rehabilitate him but it didn't work. I tried to help him remember who he was. When that failed I went to his room and tried to and find some of his old things, you know, to jog his memory. All of his belongings were gone and he had nothing but a cassette player. That's when I discovered the recording and put it all together. The warden knew full well what he was doing. Hypnosis is a powerful thing. Swiped his mind clean. Conditioned him."

"I don't know what to make of this place," said Norton.

"The best of it," said Otto, "That's all you can do. Pass your time by searching for arrowheads in the yard or playing harmless jokes on other residents. Keep your nose clean, most importantly."

"But there has to be something that can be done. Something should be done. How can he get away with running a place so cruel as this?"

"Don't think like that. It's dangerous," said Otto, wishing he never brought up the disparity of the place, wishing that someone else exposed Norton and Chub to the truth, that they found out on their own.

"Someone needs to call the authorities. And what about letters? Christ, someone should send a letter to congress."

"Won't work."

"Ten letters," said Norton, "Fifty letters. A hundred, however many it takes."

"For starters, I don't think any resident has ever made a call out of here. They claim there is no service. No telecommunication towers. No phone lines within a forty mile radius. As for the letters, we do get incoming mail, but only in the form of social security checks and retirement. For those of us who had a retirement."

"But you're the man who knows how to get things? If there's anybody that can figure out how to make contact with the outside it should be you."

"Listen, getting things from the outside is easy. If you ever want something you don't have to go through me, you can just go straight to the man himself. The person I'm talking about is Charlie Oslo. He's the security guard that patrols the yard and randomly checks rooms. Bloke will do anything for a dollar. He doesn't let anything leak out beyond these walls, though. I've been giving him letters addressed to family for years. I've yet to receive a word. You would think my daughter, or grandson or Uncle or somebody would have written me back by now. What he does with the letters I do not know."

"I see," Norton's head hung low, "I'm sorry."

Just then a loud knock could be heard on the door. Then it was followed by two more, 'KNOCK! KNOCK!'

Otto up and scrambled his way to the peephole. He feared that maybe the Warden or Badger had been listening to their conversation.

"I think it's Badger!" he whispered, his eye still stuck to the glass orb.

"I can hear you Otto. Let me in."

"I think he's angry," said Chub.

"It's okay," said Otto, trying to sound calm. Taking a deep breath, he opened the door.

The two just stood there in the doorway looking at each other.

"Well?" Choctaw said.

"Oh yes, right, I almost forgot," said Otto, exhaling another sigh of relief.

Norton studied Choctaw's arm and could tell it was starting to revert back to a normal color again. The swelling was beginning to subside. He then pondered the question of why Choctaw clutched a bundle of dried out limbs.

"Norton, Chub, follow us. Otto and I have something we want to show you."

CHAPTER EIGHT

Walking out into the courtyard, the dusk air set cool on their skin and the crunch of rocky ground could be heard beneath their feet. Choctaw dropped the dried limbs, each of which made a hollow thump against the other.

They were looking at a circular pit lined with river rocks and the coals of a fire that was fighting to stay alive. Choctaw pulled a tightly wound bundle of dead weeds out of a pouch hanging off his right hip. Placing them over the coals, a flame curled upwards to the sky. Norton and Chub watched as he placed each limb, arranging them in a way that seemed quintessential to everything a fire needs.

"Most people just throw wood into a pit, add some type of tinder, and that's their fire," Choctaw said. "By stacking wood in this way, your firewood will last twice as long. The gaps between each limb are so the fire can breath, but the real key, is making sure the fire isn't breathing too much. On a windy day, I would have just laid each limb on top of the other. I would have had no gaps. It's not a hard concept, but few people know how to make a warm and efficient fire."

"What is this?" Norton asked, "The boy scouts?"

Choctaw winced. "Fire is a gift from the Creator, Norton, the manifestation of spirit. In the days of old, fire was used to warm our homes, cook our food, show us our way through the night."

"You know what else was a gift from the creator?" Norton asked.

"What?"

"Thomas Edison."

Choctaw looked down and shook his head, his voice giving off the tone and cadence of refined wisdom, or at-least trying to. "Do not forsake the primal. You and it have far too much in common."

Norton looked at him sideways. One of his eyebrows was perched higher than the other.

"You see how this limb is turning gray?"

"Yes."

"It is like you Norton. Like an old man."

Otto chuckled with Norton and Chub.

"This, Norton, is a sacred fire. We are to treat it gently as if it were an elder."

Norton snorted.

"When you find yourself struggling, know that it will be out here in the courtyard, constantly burning. It is a place to send prayers up with the smoke." Otto, Chub, and Norton had been looking deep into the fire, caught by its dynamic and life-full glow. Choctaw, however, was bouncing his glance between the fire and the emerging stars. Occasionally, he would look to Norton and Chub as he spoke.

"Some time ago," said Otto, "when the natives still ran free, many of them had sacred fires like we have here. Tribes and chiefdoms would appoint a keeper of the fire, a position held in high honor. If the tribe ever had to move, the keeper would carry coals in a log from one camp to the next, always being sure to keep the fire alive. To let the fire die was a grave mistake, sometimes resulting in the death of the keeper."

Otto smiled and looked at Choctaw, who nodded in approval.

"Each week, a keeper is appointed amongst the residents. Chub, I think you have it next week."

Chub tilted his head up and pointed at himself, "Me?" he asked nervously.

"Don't worry Chub, we are a lot more relaxed than the Indians used to be. If the fire goes out on your watch, just come get Choctaw or me. We'll help you to get it going again, without injury," he smiled. The tone of his voice was reassuring, and, a slight but noticeable change could be seen in Chub's posture, as if the pride of assuming an honorable duty had been recognized.

"I'm surprised the Warden allows this," said Norton.

"He uses the fire to burn files," said Otto.

"No telling what kinds of sins those files contain. Makes me furious." Choctaw's brow-ridge was pinched together, expressing contempt. "You're not supposed to throw trash in the sacred fire."

"Choctaw, what is your real name?" Norton asked.

"Yuma, which translates to son of the chief."

"Has it ever bothered you? I mean, has the nickname ever got under your skin?"

"No. Of course not," said Choctaw. "I've considered it an honor to be called after the people of my tribe. I suppose Otto is playing fun with my heritage, and I do see what you mean, but I am not the sensitive type. I understand that Otto cannot help the overly sporty characteristics so common amongst short men of European dissent."

Norton started laughing, surprised by Choctaw's cleverness. "What brought you here," he chuckled again, "...to Dave Springs?"

"Now, this is a subject which I am sensitive about," he said, "...but I will tell you."

Norton noticed Choctaw's face assume a burden not previously there. He felt sorry and could tell he touched on something that troubled Choctaw deeply.

"I'll never forget it. I was taking my Grandson out to show him the mound where those of his ancestral line are supposed to lay. The mound is small and barely noticeable to the untrained eye. It has been weathered a bit over the years and now resembles a hill, but it is *not* a hill. When we came up on the site, a straight red line had been painted on the ground. It crossed the middle of the mound and stretched out in either direction for as far as we could see. Orange flags were placed at specific intervals along the line. Printed on each were the words *Steelco Natural Gas*."

Norton sincerely wished he was not about to hear what he knew was coming.

Choctaw continued, "The Government granted approval for the line, even though archaeological surveys were still underway. Rushing back home I immediately made phone calls to the tribal counsel. Later that week I went out to the mound and was shocked to find myself greeted by construction workers. The supervisor on sight instructed that I stay back, that I was on public property and that, 'sir, at the moment, this mound does not belong to you or your ancestors, but rather to the state of Oklahoma.' The supervisor said when they encounter human remains as they had found, they are required by law to call the archaeological firm so further assessments can be made. 'I already have one of my men filling out the paperwork,' he told me, as the trench digger continued to rip through the ground behind him. Apparently he missed the part of the law that said construction had to cease. There was nothing I could do. I tried pressing for a legal battle, but I couldn't find a lawyer who cared. A few acted like they did. Not much ever came out of them, though."

"So what did you do?" Chub asked.

"I followed the pipeline into Texas. Walked four hundred miles, determined to catch up with the crew. I slashed tires and poured sawdust in their gas tanks. Even set fire to three backhoes."

"Wow."

"I imagine that's what they said when they walked out the next morning to resume work, that and a good deal more."

"How did you get caught?"

"The supervisor's truck had a company emblem on the door, but all the other trucks were plain white. I knew because I had seen him driving it around back in Oklahoma. I wanted him to know why his equipment got sabotaged. I didn't want him to think it was a senseless act of vandalism. Being old as I am, with death not far off anyway, I cloaked myself in ceremonial dress and leaned against his truck until morning, a double-barreled shotgun strapped around my chest. None of the crew dared come within a hundred yards. When the police arrived I laid down my gun and cooperated."

The long conversation that followed somehow managed to chart every subject from ancient Indian tales to famous prison escapes and the best restaurants they ever ate at. But the conversation eventually grew weary and all that could be heard was the crackling of the fire. The four silently observed as one of the limbs broke and succumbed to the coals below. Otto raised his wristwatch and pressed a button, illuminating the face. "I think I'm gonna go back to my room," he said, "It's been a day, gentlemen." He looked to the sky before turning to depart, "Oh, Norton and Chub," he said, stopping, "If you hear something scampering across the floor in the middle of the night... nevermind it, only a rat."

*****

That night Norton could feel the weight hanging beneath his eyes. Thoughts were dashing around his head and he knew he needed to calm them for sleep. They were coming and passing as screenplays. Instead of being an active participant of his experience, he was now some omnipresent observer, watching from afar as he and Chub rocked to and fro on the bus ride in, the music still ringing in his ears and the heat still warm within his skin. He was with Otto and Chub again as they toured the grounds and stumbled into Choctaw. The scene of the snakes fang piercing Choctaw's hand replayed over twice, then three times more. In a sleepy and half-neurotic state, Norton walked through the Marijuana factory, thinking it to be a much larger and never-ending place.

He then wondered about Chub, who was in the next room over, retracting into a corner across from his bed, staring at the pink stain on the floor as though it were rising up and coming alive, his gut churning over a sense of doom. Chub thought of moving towards the bed, but only because it would be illogical to stand in the corner all night. His feet ached and his back was sore. He lacked the endurance such a feat would require. *There's no stains in the main room,* he thought, *maybe I could sleep on the floor in there?* Of course, just when this seemed a more appealing option than the unkempt bed, he remembered what Otto said about the rats. *Maybe it's best I'm off the floor,* he thought, making his way to the nightstand and flipping on the lamp. Apprehensively, he grabbed the sheets with two fingers and began to pull them back slowly.

As his weight bore down on the bed a spring popped through the mattress and punched his side. Screeching, he rolled over and grabbed at the pain. This is exactly what he expected. He knew the bed was unfit for duty. *A cot would beat this,* he thought, wondering if Norton's bed was equally as rough. Deep down he wished it would be. *Wouldn't be fair otherwise.* He then wondered if the rest of the residents had bad beds. Surely his own luck wasn't so bad as to be the only one with a rough bed. There had to be others.

Norton rolled over to turn off his lamp when a pen on his nightstand caught his attention. He noticed the silver pen the day before, but he didn't give it much thought. It was a fountain pen, the kind with a sharp end. Seizing it firmly in his hand, he scratched a tally mark downwards into the wood. A long shaving curled up underneath the pen's head before falling behind the bed. Carefully, he carved another mark for day two then set the pen on the nightstand. Fixing his foggy gaze upon the marks, he could feel consciousness began to fade. Using what energy he had remaining, he twisted the small black knob on the lamp, hearing it click once, then twice. The room went dark. A scampering noise made its way across the floor, barely registering in his mind, for he was off to sleep.

*****

Before Norton knew it he was waking up to a headboard full of tally marks. What had started as a tiny sliver of wood beneath his bed had now turned into a pile of shavings. The head on the fountain pen, once sharp, was worn down to a stub. That morning he simply lay there staring at the ceiling fan. It rotated around with a slight wobble in its orbit, the blades spinning slow enough to follow, a bronze pull chain rocking back and forth.

No reason existed for him to get out of bed and he assumed it well to skip breakfast. By lunch he figured Otto or Chub might wonder where he had been. To his disappointment, no one seemed to notice.

Lunch went as it normally did, everyone sat in the same seat as the day before that and the day before that, as if some unspoken rule existed that forbid them from sitting anywhere different. Fran stood over in the corner by the windows.

"I'm tired of porridge," said Norton, looking down at his plate. "Porridge for breakfast, porridge for lunch, porridge for dinner..."

"Yeah," said Chub. He was thinking of a good barbeque sandwich from Jaivon's, the thick-bodied smell of oaks and caramels wafting off the smoked meat right before he took a bite. "I miss selling ice cream. We had some nice times in that Wal-Mart parking lot, treating people to ice cream and barbeque with Jaivon. I always liked the birds. Wal-Mart birds not scared a lick. They come rights to ya."

"Me too," said Norton, "Me too." He was thinking of their houseboat, wondering if the homeowners association had foreclosed on it yet. His mind then turned to their friend Duffy and his vibrant yellow hot air balloon. Norton imagined Duffy high in the sky, the large smiley face floating above the city of Phoenix.

"Say," said Otto, "You guys noticed Frankie and Gomez?"

"I don't like them," said Chub, his speech tense and worried. "I really, really don't like them."

"They've been looking over here a lot more lately," said Otto, staring back at Frankie and Gomez, who held sly and perverted looking grins, their gaze in the direction of Norton, Otto and Chub. "I think maybe they're planning something. What I don't know..."

"Have you ever thought of—" Norton paused, leaning in towards Otto "trying to escape?" he finally asked.

"Escape? Where to? So what if you do make it beyond the razor wire. Then what? We're over one hundred miles away from the nearest town. Nothing but desert."

"I like the idea," said Chub, staring down at the watery porridge running into his corn. It certainly wasn't the kind of meal he was used to on the outside. "It stinks in here. And... some of these people I wonder about, Norton."

Norton noticed Chub looking past him towards the end of the table. He turned around to see what Chub was staring at. Badger appeared to have been listening intently to their conversation. At Norton's glance, he looked down and resumed eating.

"Where do Frankie and Gomez get their clothes from anyway?" Norton asked, staring back at Frankie and Gomez now, thinking little of Badger. The two men always sat at the women's table, namely because that's precisely what they wanted to be. They wore Sunday gowns that appeared several sizes too small but still too big to fit on any of the other ladies. Frankie and Gomez were also the only people in the entire home that made use of the exercise bench in the courtyard. Their builds were no longer muscular per-say, but they were still big and not in the flabby sort of way.

"I have no idea," said Otto. "One has to wonder, though."

"What were we saying?" Norton asked, "Right, escape…. I think it might be possible."

"And what when you get out?" Arm Pit asked in an off-putting tone. "You'll be considered a convict. To leave here would be like breaking parole or something worse, probably something worse."

"Never mind. Forget I mentioned it," Norton rose from the table. "You can stay here."

"Wait," said Badger, grabbing Norton firmly by the arm, his hand slipping down loosely to grasp Norton's. Upon the touch, the nerves in Norton's palm sent out an unexpected sensation. Instead of feeling the skin on Badger's hand, he was feeling what seemed to be a paper napkin.

Badger was trying to give him something.

CHAPTER NINE

Chub wished he were down on floor forty-eight again, spraying fertilizer with the heavy packs, anything but this. The conveyor belt was the most painful task in the patch, far more painful than stacking, packaging or fertilizing, although, fertilizing was painful enough. As usual Chub worked alongside Otto and Norton; the Warden having realized early on that the three worked well together. To be sure, without Otto around in the factory, Norton held a gloomy attitude and worked slower than usual. Without Norton or Otto, Chub simply didn't work at all.

The three men sifted through buds as they zoomed by on the conveyor belt, their arms dancing around hysterically in an attempt to pick out seed and stems. A sharp and inescapable pain in the lower back always accompanied this work. One was forced to lean over the conveyor in order to reach the buds at the center. Norton and Chub were told this pain would go away after the first week. "Your body gets used to it," said the Warden, but how would he know, he never actually worked the belt, he just stood in occasionally, making sure all the seeds and stems were being picked.

Norton always grumbled when on the belt, bickering about how they needed to slow it down. This was true. Every machine in the factory was tuned to operate at the limits of human capability. It was barely possible to catch all the seeds and stems before they dropped off and went to packaging. The Warden seemed to enjoy storming around the factory and spitting in people's ears, informing that they were too slow and falling behind, his rage mounting as the day wore on and the residents grew fatigued.

"What do you think you're doing?" The Warden yelled as Norton bobbled over seeds and stems.

Him again...? Norton thought, wanting to yell the words *Screw off!* This was the fourth time the Warden had been over to bark down his back. In truth, he was doing a worse job than usual, his mind preoccupied by thoughts of escape and the note Badger slipped into his hand at lunch. *But hell,* he figured, *I'm working for free, what does he expect?*

Carrying on conversation was hard. Machines spun at high RPM's and everyone who had yet to lose their hearing wore ear buds.

"Ahh!" yelled Frankie, grabbing at his ear and throwing himself on the floor.

Chub watched as a wax smeared ear bud hit the ground and rolled under one of the machines. Frankie bent over, his blouse stretched taught, a long slit shearing up the rear. What was revealed in this tear of clothing neither Chub nor Norton wanted to see, but see they did. The cheeks were ridden with cellulite, sagging over the back of his thighs. They looked like tear drop shaped water balloons about to burst. Norton and Chub made a revolting jerk in the opposite direction and let out a shrill. Otto, surprised by their sudden unrest, turned to—

"Oh my God!" he let out a cry.

Gomez and Frankie were both giggling uncontrollably, their faces flushed bright pink. As Frankie pressed himself off the floor he made little attempt to cover this rearmost window to the world. Otto quickly tried to find something to speak of, his mind scrambling for anything to separate it from the sight it just saw.

"What did Badger write on that napkin anyway?

"What?" Norton asked, remembering he had the napkin in his pocket and that he still didn't know what to do with it. He was slightly astonished Otto managed to notice.

"So what does it say?"

"I'm not sure I can tell you," said Norton, "I mean... obviously whatever it is, it's supposed to be between me and Badger."

"Come on. Seriously. After all I've done for you guys."

"You're gonna hold that over me?" Norton asked, struggling with whether or not he should tell Otto what was on the napkin. *Otto might be able to give me some advice,* he thought to himself, finally unfolding the napkin and handing it to Otto. Chub quickly perched himself over Otto's shoulder and read what it said.

Tomorrow Night.

The cemetery.

2:15 A.M.

"Interesting," said Otto.

Chub shrunk back to his end of the conveyor belt, staring off towards a wall but looking past it.

"There's no way I'm going to meet that man in the cemetery," Norton said. "I could tell he likes you, actually. I'm not sure why but he does. I doubt he means any harm."

"Either way, I've got no business in a cemetery at two. Neither does he."

"It makes sense now..."

"What? What makes sense Otto?" Chub asked desperately.

"He's had a lot of dirt underneath his fingernails lately. He's constantly trying to keep them clean. Carries around a fingernail clipper everywhere he goes."

"He's a graverobber," said Norton.

"Or he's trying to escape," said Otto. "I think he's tunneling his way out."

"He did seem," Norton paused, "interested in our conversation about escaping."

"I'm curious," said Otto, "Whatcha say we sneak out to the cemetery tonight, get there before he does? I know of a good place to hide."

"What're you guys talking bout?" Choctaw asked while passing by, curious as to the conversation the three seemed so intent on.

"Choctaw," said Otto, "you visit the cemetery regularly. Have you—"

Norton jeered into Otto's side, scared he might spill the news to Choctaw too.

"Have you seen anything, er... out of the norm?"

"No. Not really. Well, actually, yes. Yes I have."

Otto looked over at Norton and Chub, then down at the ground, pondering what Choctaw might be about to say.

"As I entered the cemetery gate last Tuesday, I noticed what appeared to be a slight depression in the dirt. You can follow it all the way to Old Man Parkins."

"Aha!" said Norton, looking at Otto, "The tunnel collapsed."

"Tunnel?" Choctaw asked.

This time it was Otto who jeered Norton in the side. Norton straightened up, acknowledging his spoof.

"This... um, depression," Otto nodded Choctaw onward, pressing for more information.

"He's been getting a lot of visitors, Old Man Parkins," said Choctaw. "The strange thing is, I don't know by whom. I haven't actually seen anyone visit his grave, nor have I seen any ornaments or wreaths placed on it. But somebody has to be visiting him. A foot trail is something that requires a serious amount of traveling."

Norton rolled his eyes and nearly collapsed in the weight of his sigh, "It's just a foot trail."

Chub spoke up hopefully, a jubilant grin spread thinly across his lips and into his dimples. "Maybe Badger wanted to introduce Norton to his old friend Mr. Parkins. Maybe that's why he wanted to meet in the cemetery."

Norton gave Chub a jab to the rib, but it was too late. The secret was no longer containable.

"Badger?" Choctaw asked. "You think Badger is the one who's been visiting Old Man Parkins?"

"No," said Otto, "We think he is up to something more. But—"

"Get back to work!" The Warden roared from across the factory. The four men instantly picked up speed at the conveyor belt, now giving at-least half of their attention to the sticky buds passing by.

"Choctaw and I are climbing on the roof later tonight," said Otto. "You two should come. We can finish this conversation there."

"The roof?" Norton asked, his mind wandering over the potential it might have for an escape route.

"Yeah," said Otto, "The roof. I missed the Geminid meteor shower last year. I'm not missing it again."

"Well..." said Norton sardonically, "Maybe we'll ride off on one when it passes."

*****

After two unsuccessful attempts to climb the ivy lattice on the south wall of the courtyard, Chub wanted to head back to his room and leave Norton on top of the roof with Otto and Choctaw.

"You'll be fine," said Norton.

"Easy to say. You're not the one who fell ten feet onto your head."

"Stop being a wimp. You didn't land on your head," said Norton. "And you were only on the third rung when it broke."

All Chub could see was their heads looking down from the side of the roof. Choctaws long hair hung below him. Chub thought the sight to be funny. Not wanting to be left out, he decided to give the climb one more go. Every move felt harrowing and took nerve, especially the last part where he had to throw his leg over and onto the roof. Had it not been for the aid of Choctaw pulling him upwards by the belt, he was certain he would have crashed hard on the ground below.

There, the four old men stood gazing into infinity, the sky an inky black and checkered with clouds, a crescent moon peaking through only occasionally, teasing their human appetite for beauty. In order to place the barbwire fence and parking lot out of sight, they decided to lie down on their backs. Their view now panoramic, a small meteor pierced the night sky.

After Norton counted nine shooting stars, and Otto argued it was actually eleven, Choctaw had a revelation he felt the urge to share. "If you stop and think about it," he said, "we are the mind, the soul, and the heart that gives the cosmos a beat."

The other three responded with a simultaneous, "Huh?"

"Well," Choctaw went on, "Some of us may swim, others walk, a few crawl or fly, but we're all natives to the same universe. The elements that make up a bird, or a rock, or a star or anything can be found in each of us. We're all made of the same stuff. We, here in this present moment, speaking and sharing thoughts with one another; are we anything less than pieces of the universe conversing with itself?"

Norton got up and walked over to the edge at the front of the building. "We could string together some type of rope ladder, simply scale down the front of the building."

Choctaw spit in front of his feet, bothered by Norton's failure to be enlightened.

"And the barbed wire fence?" Chub asked.

"I'll think of something."

"I don't like the idea of climbing a barbed wire fence."

"Who said we have to climb it? We could cut it; go through it. I certainly like the idea a lot better than Badgers tunnel."

"Forget it," said Otto. "There are motion detectors down there. You'll trigger the alarm and the dog will be on you before you even get your cutters out."

"Dog?" Norton asked.

"See that over there?"

Norton and Chub peered out with squinting eyes and studied what Otto pointed at. It was a small doghouse, painted black, the words Hannibal written in blood red above the door.

"That's why Badger's plan actually stands a chance," said Otto. "If his tunnel takes him beyond the wire, he'll bypass the alarm and have time to put some distance between himself and Hannibal."

"But we don't know if Badger's digging a tunnel. And I'm not crazy about crawling into one either. And if he is digging a tunnel, where is he putting all the excess dirt?"

"I don't know," said Otto, curling his mustache with a finger, "that's something I've been trying to figure out."

"If you ever end up in the Warden's office," said Choctaw, "which I hope you don't. You'll notice a shelf behind his desk that is lined with shoes. They are worn and ratty and bear scars all over. Oslo, his guard, told me they were the shoes of those who came before us, the shoes of those unable to outrun Hannibal."

Norton felt a weighty mass rolling down his throat. His plan was not an option. "What do the inspectors think of the shoes? Surely this place gets inspected; surely they have to ask about the shoes, about everything else in here. How do they not know?" Norton pleaded, feeling unjustified by the system.

"Oh, they don't go near that office," said Otto, "The Warden has an entirely different office in Wing A. What you have seen of the home is only Wing B. The inspectors never see Wing B. Every time they come through, the Warden always takes his favorite residents over to Wing A. Bunch of suck ups who pretend as if the home is pleasant and things are okay. The Warden will repay them for their service with gifts of different sorts. I don't know much about Wing A, but I've been told the rooms are immaculately kept and even have air conditioning. They also have their own showers."

"What a farce," said Norton disgusted.

"Hey guys," Chub whispered quietly under his breath. "I think I see something heading towards the home; off over there, on the horizon."

The three others lifted their heads and saw the long ray of headlights shining far off across the desert floor. Before long, a semi-truck could be seen rocking back and forth on the bumpy road that led up to the home. When it arrived at the gate and stopped, a dust cloud over ran the truck, consuming it as the breaks let out a squeal.

Right then the Warden could be seen walking into the courtyard. "Stay Hannibal," he snarled loudly.

Walking towards the truck's headlights, his shadow grew longer and longer behind him. Opening a box at the gate, he pulled a lever down and a faint '*beep*' could be heard. The gate opened.

Oslo emerged from beneath their lookout. He started waving the driver to come in, and then proceeded to back him up to the front doors right beneath them. When the truck was but several meters from the front doors, Oslo threw chocks in front of the tires to keep it from rolling forward. The driver, leaving the truck running, stepped down to meet the Warden.

Up on their rooftop, the old men found themselves straining to hear the Warden speak with the driver.

"You're early," said the Warden sternly.

"Since when has that been a bad thing," the driver asked?

"You weren't supposed to be here until next Tuesday. Do you people not have a calendar or at-least half a brain?" They heard the Warden swear something else.

"I'm sorry," said the driver, "I didn't know."

"Well you should have known," said the Warden, "I'll have words with your superior and figure out precisely why you didn't, but let's get this truck unloaded shall we."

"Listen, I'm really sorry. Please don't call—"

"Pipe it!" said the Warden. "I'm pissed as it is."

"Right..." said the driver, hustling towards the back of the truck where Oslo waited. He opened the doors and disappeared into the truck. Oslo motioned someone forward that was beneath the purview of the old men. A forklift drove out from inside the building as a pallet was wheeled up to the edge of the semi trailer.

Otto studied the pallet, trying to make out what they were about to ship into the building. From their height he could not quite tell, but the Warden spoke and gave him a clue. "Benjamin Franklin would be proud," he said, staring over the stacks of green on the pallet.

"Yes, and there are more Franklins, much more," said the driver. "Business is going well on the outside."

"Good," said the Warden. "That might be your saving grace. But if I ever see you without notice again—"

"Yes Sir," said the driver, his voice shaken.

"Yes Sir?"

"I mean, no Sir. You won't see me unannounced again. I'm not sure how you missed word, but it shouldn't, I mean," the driver paused, "It won't happen again."

"Good," said the Warden. He then nodded toward Oslo and walked back inside.

The four men were struck by what they saw unfolding below. Had the Warden looked up at that particular time, there is no doubt he would have seen their jaws gaping outward. Speechless, they watched as three more pallets were lifted from the trailer and carried into the building. Once the job was done, they pulled back from their perch and sat there, saying

nothing.

CHAPTER TEN

The shower seemed busier than usual and Norton made a determined effort not to pay mind to the naked bodies around him. His chest tightened in a jolt and remained constricted, the cold water running down his body reined him in on the present moment, his ears now filled with the crackle of water drops bursting below.

"Friggin freezing," said Otto through chattering teeth.

Norton chortled, "If we stay here long enough we'll have icicles between our legs."

"I think I already do," said Otto, "...certainly can't feel it."

"Have they ever had hot water in this place?" Norton asked.

"Never."

The two showered hurriedly, shutting their spigots off at nearly the same time. Otto rubbed his towel into his hair and could hear the sound of soapsuds popping. *Oh well,* he thought, *soapy hair will have to do.* Norton and Otto were dressed and waiting outside by the time Chub finished lathering up. When he exited the showers he told Norton and Otto that he'd meet them in the cafeteria.

"I have to go back to my room and change, forgot to bring a pair of clean boxers."

As soon as Chub entered the courtyard he could hear the tink of weights. *Ah, please don't notice me, don't notice me, don't notice—*

"Hey honey," came a voice to his right.

Keep walking. Keep walking.

"Hey, where you going so fast?"

Chub could feel their presence working in on him. In his mind they were beginning to salivate.

"Look here, boy," said Frankie, snatching Chub by the arm.

Desperately trying to yank away, Chub unknowingly twisted Frankie's elbow into an unnatural position. His grip broke lose and Chub made a scramble for the cafeteria, the only place he could be sure others would be.

"Want to play dirty, huh boy?"

Chub was about to pass the weight bench when Gomez pulled him down by the shoulders. As Chub began to fall he grasped for the first thing near. His hand now on a ten-pound weight, Chub managed to connect with Gomez in an ungraceful yet forceful blow. The whole situation was brought on with such suddenness that Chub was unsure of how he did it. Lying there on the ground by Gomez, Chub watched as a trickle of blood coursed it's way down the side of Gomez's face before seeping into the dirt. Frankie ran up and shook Gomez frantically, slowly jarring him back into consciousness.

"Gomez, Gomez," he cried, "Wake up! Gomez!"

"What's going on here!" yelled an unmistakable voice.

Chub watched as snakeskin boots walked up from eye-level, apparently too stunned to get back on his feet.

"Chub," the Warden asked, "Did you do that?"

"Whaah, whaah, me? I... I didn't mean..."

"Terrific," barked the Warden, "I've never liked that one, Gomez. Gives me the creeps, him and this other one. You okay?"

"Whaah, whaah, me?" Chub asked, perhaps more stunned by the Warden's concern than anything.

"Yes, here," the Warden helped Chub to his feet. "Listen, come to my office after you eat lunch. I've got a special assignment for you. Something that's uh, better than the cabbage patch."

"Right," said Chub, "I... I will. I'll be there."

The Warden kicked Gomez in the ribs and ushered him away with Frankie.

Lumbering his way towards the cafeteria, Chub found himself wishing the whole occurrence never happened. Before Frankie and Gomez only wanted a piece of him, now he feared they might want much more.

*****

Chub had relatively no food on his plate when he sat down, a telling sign for Norton and Otto that something was up. Watching him for a moment, neither of them quite knowing what to say, they noticed his hand shaking, rattling a fork against his tray. He reached for his drink and brought it splashing to his lips, a slosh of grape juice running over the side and down the glass.

"Tell me what happened," Norton demanded, but in a sincere way, his voice sounding concerned.

Chub was silent.

Norton studied his eyes and could tell they were soaking up tears like sponges.

Crying was something that Norton disdained. Chub knew this and never cried much, but he was struggling now, struggling really hard.

"It's okay, just tell us what happened..."

Chub meant to say Frankie and Gomez tried to grab him in the courtyard. All that came out was the word *Frankie.*

"Frankie and Gomez?" Norton bellowed. Chub could practically see the steam coming out of his ears. "Where are they?" Norton shouted.

"Wa, wa, warden took em off," said Chub.

"So what happened?" Otto asked, wanting to pry out an explanation as much as everyone else at the table.

Chub was beginning to gather himself up "I clobbered Gomez. Clobbered em good."

"You what?" Arm Pit asked.

"Cross the forehead with a weight," said Chub, now feeling a strange sense of pride, "Grabbed me by the shoulders."

Everyone at the table hung forward, fastened on Chub.

"Frankie ran up screaming, *Gomez! Gomez!,* and we was on the dirt, the both of us. Then the Warden was in our faces, and before Gomez became awares the Warden kicked him in the side."

"Where are they now?" Norton asked.

"The Warden took em off," said Chub.

"Oh that's not good," said Otto, a concerned look on his face.

"You think he's placing them in confinement?" Arm Pit asked.

"I'm not sure. I guess we'll know if they don't come back."

Silence came over the table as the men continued to eat, each of them mulling over what they had just been told. Norton glanced up to see Badger reach the end of the lunch line and slop porridge onto his plate. Turning around for the table he shot Norton a sportive wink.

Why, Norton thought, his gut hollowing out at once. *Why did Badger have to give me that note?*

That night, Otto, Chub and Choctaw would be following him to watch Badger in the cemetery, their suspicion being that he was digging a tunnel. Where and how is what they cared to know. Or at-least, that's what Otto cared to know when Norton agreed to spy on him. Norton assumed he would have been content staying back in his room. He could tell Badger he got sick, lost the note or didn't like cemeteries. He didn't have to go. *How foolish of me*, he thought, figuring maybe he could tell Otto he didn't feel well.

But if Badger is digging a tunnel, that might be our only way out—no, don't be stupid. Norton shook his head. *A tunnel is crazy.*

Suddenly, Norton could feel two hands latch tightly onto his shoulders from behind.

"Mr. Kranowski," spoke the voice to which the hands belonged, and Norton knew that this could only be one person—the Warden. No one else in the home called him by his last name.

Not knowing whether he should turn around, Norton sat there in an almost trance like state. The Warden began to roll his hands forward, then backward, pressing his thumbs in and around. He was giving Norton a massage, but not in the most friendly sort of way.

"You and Otto here are going to have a new task." He paused, and then added, "Possibly for the month. You'll be going to the laundry room. Typically I have Stacy and Hagrith do the laundry, but, as they've taken it upon themselves to steal bed linens for their sewing projects, they've been moved to the factory. Any questions?"

"Uh, no, none," said Norton, and with that the Warden let go of his shoulders to walk off.

"Hey, huh," the Warden spun around at the end of their table, his head darting up towards the ceiling. "You guys hear that?"

Otto surveyed everyone at the table and said, "No, didn't hear anything, sir."

The Warden's head shot around the cafeteria, his hands on edge by his hips, as though he were about to grab a side arm. "Sure?" he asked.

"I think so," said Otto.

A skeptical look came over the Warden's face and he began to make his way out of the cafeteria, a wary gait in his step.

"Believes the place is haunted," said Arm Pitt.

"And probably is," said Badger from the end of the table.

Chub swallowed his last spoonful of lunch without chewing.

Without warning a choir sang forth across the cafeteria. Grumpy was leading the women's table in a horrendous version of Amazing Grace.

"You have got to be kidding me," said Badger.

"They sound like a wounded bobcat," said Arm Pit.

Badger rose to go dump what was left on his tray.

The next person to rise was Otto and soon the rest of the men were following Badger on his way to the trash. Norton and Chub waited patiently for Otto to dump his food when they were approached by a, "High! I'm Fran, I've been certified for 53 years, 6 months, 8 days, and 43 minutes..."

Norton thought maybe a tunnel wouldn't be so bad after all.

CHAPTER ELEVEN

Leaving the cafeteria, Norton and Otto turned left up the hall for the laundry room. Chub cut right for the Warden's office.

"Keep an eye out," Norton beckoned at Chub as the three parted ways.

Chub felt queasy at the thought of Frankie and Gomez. Then there was the prospect of entering the Warden's office. This day just didn't seem to be going well.

"Ah, Chub, welcome," said Warden warmly.

Chub couldn't help but think he was being enticed into some sort of trap.

"Sit down, sit down," said the Warden grabbing a chair, "Have a seat."

The first thing Chub noticed was the shoe rack. Measuring about six feet long and perched high on a wall behind the Warden's desk, the plank of wood was polished to a sheen and packed end to end. Some of the shoes sat there in pairs, others were missing either their left or right counterpart, but all of them were a shredded mass of teeth marks. Chub recalled Otto telling them about the Warden's dog while they were on the rooftop.

"I like you Chub, I do," the Warden was saying. "You're the kind of guy a man can count on. I can tell. That's why I've recruited you and no one else. You should feel special, privileged, even." The Warden looked out his window, "Yes, while everyone else sweats away in the factory or washes their sweaty clothes, you'll be in here, in the air conditioning, helping me sort through all of my files."

Chub turned his attention to a vent in the ceiling. Purple yarn hung down from it, swaying in the breeze. *A vent that actually works,* Chub thought to himself.

"I have a lot of these files, so you'll be happy to hear there's enough to keep you busy and out of the factory for quite some time."

Chub turned his thoughts to the pile of folders on top of the desk.

"I ask that you go through each of these," said the Warden, picking up one of the folders from the mountainous stack. "You'll look for every instance of my name, and when you find it, you'll make sure that it disappears forever. That fire outside? Any document or receipt that has my name on it will go into the fire. Understood?"

Chub shook his head up and down, feeling his tongue had been paralyzed.

"I've already started a burn pile here," said the Warden, pointing down at a cart behind his desk that was half full of documents and folders. "When this is full you'll wheel it out to the courtyard and dump it into that fire Choctaw is so obsessed with."

Chub crossed his eyes and saw his nose. He wanted to tell the Warden how pissed Choctaw got when he dumped files in the fire.

"What did I just say?" The Warden asked menacingly, causing Chub to straighten up in his seat.

"You want me to burn the files, all the ones that have your name on em..." Chub almost asked a question, an air of uncertainty in his voice, as if this might have been the wrong answer.

"You're brilliant, Chub. Downright genius. That's it exactly!"

Chub felt relieved. Hesitantly, he reached for one of the files.

"Oh, and Chub," said the Warden on his way out the door, "If you mention anything about these files to the others, I'll be very angry. And do you want to know why I'll be so angry?"

"Uh, no. I mean yes," said Chub, unsure as to what the appropriate response would be.

"Because I've ran out of room on my shoe rack. And I *don't* want to make another one."

Chub turned his attention back toward the haggard shoes, a stiff lump rolling down his throat. When the Warden left he began sorting through the stack, chucking each document with the Warden's name into the cart. *The air conditioned room does feel nice*, he thought, his mind wandering over to what Norton and Otto might be doing.

*****

"The muskiness is unbearable," said Norton. "Sheeww!"

Otto held a pair of extra large underwear up towards the ceiling, examining a yellow stain that encircled the crotch.

"Half of these undies are still moist," said Norton, "Maybe we should throw them back in the dryer."

"I'm thinking maybe we should throw them back in the washer," said Otto, still staring at the piss stain.

Norton wrapped his arms around as many of the undies as he could and slung them into the dryer behind him. He then bent over to pick up the stragglers that were either dropped or left behind.

"At-least we don't have to hand wash," said Otto. "Imagine that. Washboards and soap bars, a day spent rubbing out poop stains."

*****

The day wore on and Chub became aware of a stinging sensation within his eyes. Reading the fine print of so many documents, he found, was both figuratively and literally painstaking, far from the break the Warden touted it would be. Chub kept finding himself rubbing his eyes and having to stand up so as not to fall asleep. Occasionally, though, something would catch his attention.

Mr. Dave Springston,

As your accountant, I am inclined to inform you of my dissatisfaction with your conduct. I am uncertain of the nature by which you operate Dave Spring's, but I can assure you, whatever it is you are doing will not go unnoticed for long.

According to the books turned over by your previous accountant, Mr. James T. Bennett, there is a three hundred thousand dollar discrepancy located quite conveniently in the expenditures section of form I-49. This is something of which I cannot easily ignore.

In conjunction with this finding, a number of other fraudulent 'errors' appear to be present in the documents you have sent me.

This letter serves as my resignation.

Sincerely,

"How are we?" The Warden asked, entering the room, causing Chub to jump.

"I've taken three loads to the fire," said Chub, his voice sounding drained.

"Well, I guess this will do for today, but don't expect every day to be this easy. Tomorrow I expect you to go through six loads. You should have it down by now."

Chub felt as though six loads was unachievable, yet he knew better than to say anything.

CHAPTER TWELVE

"Let us begin," said the Warden, addressing the residents in the Bingo Hall. "There are a few announcements I need to make before—"

"Speaking of announcements," said Grumpy, "We deserve a new water heater. The showers are cold. I get goose bumps. And you should let us ladies cook sometime. Why, we can do much better than the staff..."

"Grumpy," said the Warden, "This is not an open forum."

"And our bug problem?" Grumpy asked. "We need an exterminator."

"Grumpy. This is not—"

"You should also know that someone has been stealing our puzzle pieces."

Norton, Chub and Otto snickered. Not only was there a framed unicorn in the lobby missing an ear, but they had since removed several pieces out of each puzzle box.

"It's not right" Grumpy continued, "Something needs to be—"

"Get her out of here," said the Warden. Oslo walked over and grabbed Grumpy by the arm. She tried to yank out of his grasp but he gripped down tighter. Grumpy looked to be in pain and stood up to be escorted out the door.

"As I was saying," said the Warden, "The statin pills some of you have been receiving will be changing colors. The new statin pill is purple, but rest assured it is the same medicine, albeit a different brand. We made the switch because this brand is more er—economical."

With Grumpy gone, no one voiced any more concerns. The residents typically cared little of the weekly meetings, which were always held before the bingo wheel was spun. They each looked upon the Warden patiently, their bingo cards in hand, waiting for the Warden to get on with what they came for.

"We're dealing with a prestigious amount this evening," said the Warden as he walked over to stand behind the wheel. "It's been some time since the pot got up this high. Well, I hope everyone is ready. Here it goes!" And with that he gave the wheel a mighty spin. He always seemed to enjoy spinning it as fast as possible. Maybe he got off on seeing the residents wait eagerly for it to stop, their eyes big in the hopes that they would be the next to call bingo.

Otto checked his watch twice before the wheel finally started to lose speed. Gradually it slid round and round, until finally, it came to a slothful stop. The hatch opened. A ball rolled out.

"Bingo!" Otto shouted, right as the ball rolled into the palm of the Wardens hand. Everyone began to stir in their seat, fearful that Otto had won, hoping that there was some mistake.

"The Warden hasn't even called out the number yet," cried someone from the back of the room.

"I caught a glimpse of the number as it rolled down the shoot," Otto replied in a cool voice, knowing he saw no such thing.

The Wardens palm was closed over the ball, and everyone, including Otto, held still with anticipation. Peeking into his hand, but keeping it cuffed so the residents couldn't see, the Warden smiled and asked, "Okay, Otto. If you saw the number, then what is it?"

"Er…" Otto hesitated. He was searching for a way to sound candid. "It looked like a twenty-three," he said finally.

The Warden smiled but was slow for words. Chub and Norton slid to the edge of their seats. "That is a shame, then," said the Warden, a smirk on his face. He gave a long pause. "A shame because while you have won, all these others have lost!" He laughed, "Congratulations, Otto. You've done it again."

"This is bullshit!" said Badger. He was ripping his card into pieces as he stood up. He threw the scraps forward and over the heads of those sitting in front of him. Norton shook his head smiling. This was the third time Otto had won since the night he showed them his trick.

After collecting his sum, Otto placed his thumbs under his suspenders, arched his shoulders back, and marched triumphantly out of the game hall. Norton, Chub and Choctaw followed him to his room where they sat around his dining room table, watching as he counted out three hundred and seventy six dollars.

"Highest I've ever seen the pot go," said Choctaw.

"It's corrupt," said Otto, "All an illusion. The Warden makes us think we're getting some of our retirement check, and then he gives us only one thing to spend it on. Bingo."

"Fucking Bingo," said Norton. "If we ever escape, I'm going to expose the Warden for all he's worth... God, I never thought I would say this, but I hope Badger really is digging that tunnel."

"There's only one way to find out," said Otto. "Only one way to find out."

*****

They were kneeling in a patch of bamboo, their old knees aching on the hard Arizona ground. A few of the tombstones were leaning awkwardly, but they were all of the same shape and size. Each one was rectangular and flat on the top, not rounded as tombstones typically are. Otto kneeled there thinking they had no appeal.

"Finally," said Norton, when the silhouette of a figure could be seen at the gate, "I think that's him".

"I'm uncomfortable," Chub muttered.

"We're all uncomfortable," said Choctaw, attempting to move himself into a more desirable position.

A stalk at the top of the bamboo patch shook and Badger stopped walking. "I must need a cigarette," he thought to himself, his eyes squinting toward the top of the stalk.

The four hideouts focused in on the little flame, then the click of his zippo closing, and finally the small red ember that grew brighter with every pull.

Otto watched curiously and thought Badger's walk to be peculiar. He seemed to be walking with a happy prance in his step.

"I could swing for one of those right now," Norton whispered as Badger posted up on a tombstone and savored his cigarette.

Otto felt a sting and slapped his leg.

Badger heard Norton make the unmistakable sound of a "*Shhhh!*" Holding his pose unflinchingly, Badger casually attended to his cigarette.

A moment passed and they felt calm again. Otto murmured back apologetically, "Mosquito."

They could hear nothing but their breath and thought themselves invisible, yet Badger was all the more wise. Sitting there, he pondered the different ways in which he could handle his newfound audience. Once the cigarette reached the filter line, he flicked it out into the darkness.

"He's coming this way," Chub whispered anxiously, "Should we run?"

"No. Be patient," said Otto, "We shouldn't give ourselves away."

Badger got closer, and then closer still, stopping to sit on the last tombstone before the bamboo patch. "Brought the whole team I see. Not much for keeping secrets are ya Norton?"

"He caught us!" One of them said.

"Shhh," came Norton.

"Why *shoosh*," Badger asked? "I'm right here. I can hear you—even see you through the stalks. You're a pitiful a bunch. Caught red handed. Couldn't even keep your head down for ten minutes."

Badger got up as if his onlookers were never there and began walking back to the grave of Old Man Parkins. The four men sat behind their cover for a second longer, but, realizing the absurdity of it and driven by curiosity, they slowly walked out to see what Badger was doing.

"Well, come on! Don't just stand there. Help me set this grave cover on its side." Badger could sense the hesitancy in their eyes. "If there's one thing about it. I'll make more progress tonight than ever before. With five sets of hands, we might complete the tunnel by dusk. I was shooting to be a free man by Friday, but seriously gentlemen, we can leave tonight if you choose."

"I don't like this," said Choctaw, "Disrespecting Old Man Parkins like this."

"You should of used Rick's grave," said Otto, "No one ever liked Rick."

Badger grunted as he wielded the grave cover over and onto its side. There was a square hole about four feet wide in the front wall of the grave, but to their surprise, the skeleton of Mr. Parkins was missing.

"This is outrageous," said Choctaw.

"Don't worry about Old Man Parkins," said Badger. "I moved him a few graves over. He's in a better place now."

"I might move you over a few graves."

"Eeeasy," said Otto, noticing Choctaw's fists were clenched.

Badger cracked a grin, "Now Choctaw," he said, "We all know Old Man Parkins had a thing for Mrs. Francesca."

"I think we all did," Otto started to chuckle, then halted it quickly, suppressing the humor into a grin.

"I'm leaving!" said Choctaw, making his way to the gate.

Otto turned to watch, then looked at Norton. "I'm leaving too."

Chub wondered what Norton would decide. He wanted to leave with Choctaw and Otto, to return to the safe confines of his room.

Otto's descriptions of Badger made him out to be wild and mean, yet the person Norton studied appeared open and calm.

"Looks like it's going to be the three of us," Badger said, but only after giving the two a moment to ponder their decision. Badger leaped down into the grave. Grabbing a thick rope that ran into the tunnel, he began to pull in long stretches, hand over hand. Carefully, he coiled up the excess rope by his feet, and, gasping for a breath of air, he made one last pull. A black cart came rolling out slowly. In it sat a large tub of dirt. "Take this," he paused, his chest expanding outward, "to the cellar."

Norton and Chub were kneeling over the grave, their hands on their knees.

"Here is the key," said Badger, gesturing toward Chub. "You'll need it to open the lock."

"The cellar?" Norton asked.

"Yes. That's where I dump the dirt. Now hop down here and help me lift this out of the grave."

*****

"How..." Norton huffed, "does he carry this thing?" He and Chub were clumsily making their way across the courtyard. The tub tilted and they almost lost balance. "Watch it," said Norton, nodding his head at a small hole Chub nearly stepped in.

"You know I don't have good vision at night."

"You don't have good anything," said Norton.

Arriving at the cellar door, Norton beckoned for the key. Chub patted his right front pocket and jingled his left. He then stopped to think.

"Don't tell me?"

Sticking out his tongue in concentration, he reached into the depths of a rear pocket. "Oh, here." He smiled and stretched out his palm for Norton to grab the key.

"Two fishing sinkers, a pack of breath mints, one bottle opener, a rabbit's foot, the key, and... what is this?"

Chub shrugged his shoulders.

After repeatedly trying to put the key in upside down, Chub offered to help Norton.

"I'm fine," said Norton, "I've got it." He turned the key right side up and, this time, the lock came loose.

The two rested the swinging doors on the ground and beheld a mound of dirt that sloped upwards from the cellar floor. Norton and Chub looked down in awe. They wondered for how many nights Badger must have labored, tub after tub and shovel after shovel.

"I say we just pour the dirt in from here," said Chub.

"No that won't work. We won't be able to close the doors if we do that."

"Well I don't want to go down there," said Chub, "besides, I don't plan on crawling in no tunnel either. No way."

Norton coaxed Chub along and they slipped down into the cellar, "Listen, Chub. I'm not fond of the idea myself, but—"

"What was that noise?"

The two could hear what sounded like someone talking in the courtyard. They dumped the tub and scrambled back up the mound towards the cellar entrance. "Stay down," said Norton.

"Who is it?"

"I don't know... but, oh! He sees me." Norton ducked low.

"It's just Wallie."

"Who the heck is Wallie?" Norton asked.

"I met him one day at lunch. He told me the porridge tastes better if you add pepper and four packs of sweet n' low. Wait..." Chub's mouth was gaping wide, "Is he naked?"

"Why would he be..." Norton looked up. "Yep, he's naked."

Wallie approached, his skin glistening in the moonlight, a prideful grin smeared across his face.

"Watcha guys doin' down there?" He asked upon reaching speaking distance.

"Uh, we're um..." Chub fumbled his words.

"We're taking out the trash."

"Taking out the trash? Why, I thought they came by and got everyone's trash at noon?" Wallie looked confused.

"Yes, but they forgot to get ours today" said Norton. He always had an uncanny talent for talking his way out of things. Of course, Wallie was of little concern, but both Norton and Chub knew getting caught out at this time of night would be bad, especially if they were caught helping Badger.

According to Otto, Arm Pitt was the last person to get caught breaking curfew, and to the chagrin of every resident at the home, he was slapped with mess duty for a year. "How many ounces of sweat Arm Pitt added to our daily soup is uncertain, what is not uncertain, however, is the fact that it was a disturbing amount," Otto had told them.

Neither Norton nor Chub wanted to have mess duty, and neither Norton nor Chub knew what the ramifications of attempted escape might be.

Norton spoke, "Wallie, the real question is not what are we doing, but what the hell are you doing? You're butt ass naked for God sakes!"

"I'm Peacocking."

Norton and Chub turned to one another, as friends typically do in the face of absurdity.

"Okay...? And what might Peacocking be?"

"You see that window over there," said Wallie, pointing at room 209. Norton and Chub peered out across the courtyard to see the face of Hagrith in the window. She looked back at them through the blinds, and then quickly receded into the darkness of her room. The blinds swayed back and forth.

"And how about that window over there?" This time Wallie is pointed to a room on the ground floor. Room 114. The blinds moved, a moment passed and the door opened. Out stepped a woman in a red nightdress.

"That's Stacy Quintell. She's the one who gave Old Man Parkins his heart attack." said Wallie. "Even joked about it. Said she's to die for."

"This place is berserk," said Norton, "Downright berserk."

"There's still a lot of marrow to suck out of life, Norton. For a lad like yourself, I suspect you'll do okay with the promiscuous side of Dave Springs."

Norton cringed.

"I'll teach you how to Peacock properly. I've got the process down. Have a regiment. The women know when to look for me. Though, I could use a wingman."

Norton's eyes were dilated and looking wearily across the courtyard. Chub giggled at the thought of him strutting alongside Wallie.

"Anyways," said Wallie, "I better go now."

After Wallie disappeared, Norton and Chub scampered hurriedly out of the courtyard. Once back at the cemetery, they counted each minute of an hour before Badger crawled out of the tunnel. "Men," he said, "Just two more days. We're almost there."

CHAPTER THIRTEEN

Two days passed and the home was relatively quiet. Norton and Chub had been making preparations to leave with Badger, for Friday had come, and Badger was sticking to plan. They would leave that night.

Chub struggled with what to bring and what to leave behind. There were too many things he simply did not want to part with, but Norton kept urging him to pack lighter. "All we need is water," he said, "The human body can live for thirty days without food. If it's not water or the clothes on your back then its dead weight."

"I cannot believe we are doing this," said Chub.

"Well, you need to. This is real. We are doing this. Now hurry up. We only have five more minutes."

Chub grabbed his little throw sack and the two made way for the door. There was a chill to the night air and swaths of wind were swirling around the courtyard. The stars were blotted out by a puffy cloak of clouds and a gentle rumble could be heard in the distance. Rain was coming, and from the sound of it, a thunderstorm too. When they got to the cemetery gate, a crack of lightning lit up the ground and sky. For a split second in that burst of light, Badger could be seen more clearly, but the crack was gone as soon as it had came, and he now resumed the black silhouette he was before. The three men felt a sense of pressing urgency and kept their greeting short. With little speak of the task at hand, they soon found themselves heading into the tunnel.

"Watch your feet," said Chub, coughing on the dust kicked up by Badger and Norton. Chub elected to be last going in. He reasoned it might be easier for him to back out if things got sketchy. But with Norton crawling in front of him, the beam of light that shone from Badger's headlamp was almost entirely blocked out. "Hold on!" Chub cried, "Our light. What if it goes out?"

"I just changed the batteries yesterday," said Badger.

"What if one of us gets stuck?" Chub asked, already feeling as though he were a tight squeeze.

"The other two will pull really hard."

"What if the tunnel collapses?"

"Remember the time we crawled through the long drainage pipe by Grandpa's place?" Norton was asking, trying to invoke childhood memories. "That is similar to what we are doing now. You've already done something like this before."

"Isn't that the day you got bit by the Black Widow?"

"Maybe," said Norton, now wondering if any spiders had discovered Badgers tunnel. "Never mind. Don't think about those things," he said, "In moments like these, you just don't think Chub."

"Just don't think? Well how am I supposed to do that?"

"The same way you always do."

Chub scratched his head and the three pressed onward. Except in moments where Norton asked Badger to slow down, neither of them spoke a word. Chub had been trying to look around Norton so as to keep his eyes on the light, but with Norton bobbing up and down and moving side to side it was hard to do. To call Norton's motion a crawl would be misleading. He was instead, laying on his side and trying to work his way forward with his right elbow and knee. Chub, meanwhile, adopted what he perceived to be a caterpillar technique. Laying his body out as flat as possible, Chub would drag his legs upwards and underneath him, then sprawl out and repeat the motion.

Everyone came to a sudden stop and Norton let out a loud shriek before swearing avidly. "What was that for?" He cried.

"I had something on my leg," said Badger calmly.

"So you kicked me in the face?" Norton asked.

Badger looked back, not to check and see if Norton was okay, but rather to see where the critter went. Norton and Chub found themselves blinded by Badger's headlamp.

"Move Chub move," Norton yelled! The crawling critter was a spider about half the size of Norton's palm. He attempted to get out of the spiders path, but Chub failed to move fast enough. "It's on me, it's on me," Norton said, kicking and screaming, only to realize after the fit was over that the light had gone out and darkness had consumed them. He could no longer feel the spider and worried it might be near, but his mind quickly replaced the fear of the spider with the need for light. "Badger," he said, "Stop playing around. Turn on the light."

There was silence.

"Badger?" Norton asked, his voice faltering.

"It's okay," said Badger, "I know this tunnel like the back of my hand."

Norton huffed in irritation, "Badger."

"What? I said it will be okay."

"You lied," said Chub.

"Lied?"

"Yes, you said you changed the batteries."

"Well, I suppose they were running low."

"Running low?" Chub asked in dismay.

"Yes," said Badger, "I may have taken the ones out of my TV remote."

Norton mustered his last ounce of willpower in an attempt to contain his infuriation. With his nose throbbing from Badger's kick, he wondered how he talked himself into the hole. Chub held out his hand, trying to see something, trying to see anything. They could see neither each other nor their own bodies. A peculiar type of vulnerability swept over them. There was this eery sense that they had lost their bodies entirely. All that remained, it seemed, was the bodiless consciousness that bore their own thoughts.

"Guys... I think we should turn around," said Chub.

"I'm not turning around," said Badger firmly, pressing forward to the roar of thunder.

"Stop. I think Chub is right, Badger. We need to turn around."

"There's always tomorrow night," said Chub.

"Tomorrow night?" Badger barked. "Tomorrow night I will enjoy a cold drink at the tavern of my choosing. Turn around if you wish."

Without realizing it, Norton and Chub found themselves following involuntarily. Neither of them wanted to leave Badger and entrusted that he knew the tunnel. Claustrophobia began to set in and for a while no one spoke. Their thoughts were stimulated only by the heavy thunder and the pain signals shooting from their knees. Norton noticed that Chub was breathing heavier and heavier. He wondered if Chub was beginning to hyperventilate, but just then, a ripe odor went afloat.

"Aww, that's horrible?" Chub shrieked, his windpipes shocked open.

"Baha!" Badger bellowed, "Hardship is good. It builds character."

"Builds character?" Norton quipped, "We're seventy six years old. Anything that didn't get built a long time ago isn't going to be built tonight."

"Wait," said Badger, "Stop. Did you guys hear that?"

"No. But I certainly smell it," said Norton.

"Ah, I must be hearing things." Badger paused, "In the war we had gas masks. You could have put one of those on."

"Well thanks Badger. Thanks for letting us know that really. Very kind of you."

"In complete darkness, seconds feel like minutes. It can make a man crazy."

"Badger, for Christ's sake, keep it together. You sound like you're loosing it. What in the hell are you talking about?"

"I don't know," said Badger. "I don't like the silence. Keep talking to me boys."

"I don't like the silence either," said Chub, "How long have we been crawling?"

"About an hour."

"How much longer?"

"Oh um," Badger stopped crawling, "I'm er... not sure."
He then muttered something under his breath.

"What!" Norton howled.

Badger spoke louder, "I said we're lost. I don't know where we are."

"What!" Chub bellowed, this time able to hear what Badger said.

"Look. Badger, all we have to do is turn around. Eventually we'll come out in the cemetery."

"Maybe."

"What do you mean maybe?"

"There's more than one tunnel."

"What!" Norton yells again.

"We may have taken a wrong turn. The compass I was using when I began work on the tunnel was broken. I didn't find out I was using an awry compass until mid-way through the construction. There's a tunnel that runs due east about one mile and another—"

"One mile? One mile!" Chub tried to imagine how long it must take someone to crawl that far.

"Badger, you said there's another tunnel. Where does it go?"

"There's actually six more tunnels."

"Six tunnels? Six tunnels!"

"Chub, calm down, please," said Norton, trying to keep from freaking out himself. "We're going to get out of this, all we need is—"

"I'm not sure about that," said Badger.

"Sure about what," asked Norton.

"I'm not sure we're getting out," said Badger, "I'm starting to think I was born to die in a tunnel."

Chub swore, "If Norton wasn't between me and you right now, *you* would die in this tunnel."

Norton was taken aback, surprised Chub would speak so aggressively. "Chub, shut up and put your head on straight," he said. "Let me think."

The three got quiet for but a moment.

"Alright, since we don't know what tunnel we are in... since we don't have a light... we'll just have to move backwards and hope we come out in the cemetery. That's all we can do." Badger and Chub remained quiet. Norton assumed they were thinking over what he just said, "Chub, that means you have to lead the way."

Badger and Norton were small enough to curl up and turn around to face the opposite direction, but Chub was too constrained. Begrudgingly, he started crawling backwards. At this point their elbows and knees were worn raw and every muscle agonized. They wanted desperately to stop, but stopping was not an option. If they were to make their way back to the cemetery before sunrise, they knew that they had better crawl fast. And that they did, as fast as their poor legs and arms could carry them. They crawled for what must have been thirty minutes before Chub gave out.

"I can't take it anymore," said Chub, now lying on his belly to catch a breath.

"Let's go,"

"Just a few more seconds."

"I said, let's go!"

Chub went to resume movement but noticed his right leg seemed bound by something. Reaching down, he placed his hand on something that felt like a tangled mass of roots. He pulled gently but his foot still seemed stuck. Reaching down again, he noticed his shoelaces were somehow tangled around the roots. After a failed attempt to untie the knots, Chub grew fearsome and pulled forcefully. Before he could realize what had happened, Chub was coughing on dust and an enormous weight pressed down upon him. He was buried up to his shoulders.

"Enemies!" Badger screamed out at the noise. Norton and Chub thought he was directing the language at them. "I'm coming," he yelled, "That's right! I said I'm coming and I'm going to kill everyone of ya!" Norton and Chub could hear him scrambling away from them, his voice echoing down the tunnel and mixing with the sound of thunder.

"He's went insane," said Norton, "He's lost it."

"What are we going to do, Norton? This isn't good Norton. This isn't good."

"I don't know," said Norton, "Calm down. Maybe I can dig you out."

Norton tried desperately to move the dirt bearing down on Chub's back, but with each arm full that he managed to push aside, twice as much fell from the ceiling to replace it. "I'm going to have to leave you," said Norton, "I'll get help." Norton turned back around in the tunnel while Chub protested the idea furiously. "I have no other choice, Chub, I'm sorry," he said.

"Don't leave me Norton. Don't leave me."

"Look, I'm sorry. Don't move until I come back for help okay? If it collapses anymore your dead."

Norton resumed heading back up the tunnel, placing one arm in front of the other until he came to a split. He stuck his hand out to feel around and could tell that the tunnel diverged in two different directions. After some thought, he decided to venture down the leftward path which seemed to be sloped gradually upward. Again, he placed one arm in front of the other, telling himself to just keep moving forward.

"Comrade," said Badger, his voice right in front of Norton, so close he thought he could feel Badgers breath. "Is that you?"

Moving backwards to renew some space between them, Norton wondered if Badger was still off his rockers. By now four hours of aimless wandering had passed. He thought Badger was further along and was surprised to have run up on him.

"Badger, are you okay? Yeah, it's me. It's Norton bud."

"I thought so," said Badger, "my sense of smell is getting old though. Almost bit out your throat. Then I whiffed your cologne. Had to do that once."

"Badger! Keep it together would ya!"

"Right, yes. We are near the end. Another forty feet at most. I've been resting, collecting my energy."

"Well I'm ready, let's go."

The two moved up in the tunnel until they came to a dead end.

"This is it, are you sure you're ready," Badger asked? "There may be enemies."

"Yes, I'm ready," said Norton, "get on with it."

Badger began taking chunks out of the ceiling with a small garden shovel. The two were coughing vehemently. Directly a sliver of light broke through and Badger increased his shovel strokes with heightened intensity. When the hole looked big enough, he planted his legs and burst upward with all his might. Badgers head pierced the surface, looking around like a ground mole. Norton lay down beneath him, waiting for his turn to exit.

"Run!" Badger yelped as he leapt out and into the sun above. Norton peaked his eyes over the holes edge, saddened to see that they were still within the perimeter. Suddenly, the alarm rang out across the yard and Badger made a straight line for the fence. Norton watched nervously as Hannibal shot from his lair with great speed. Long drizzles of drool stretched out behind the dog like streamers in the wind. The savageness of the hound was terrible. Norton wisely decided he would stay in the hole. Soon, Badger was mid-way up the fence with Hannibal jumping at his legs. He hung there, clenched on for his life, unable to get above the barb wire and not daring to climb down.

The Warden walked out casually. Eventually, he called the dog off and had Oslo take Hannibal away. Badger came down and the Warden promptly placed him in cuffs. Norton watched as Oslo struggled to lead Hannibal back to his doghouse, but the dog sniffed around veraciously, barking towards the hole. Before Norton could scramble back into the tunnel, his head was spotted sticking up over the edge.

"You've got about three seconds," said the Warden hoarsely.

CHAPTER FOURTEEN

There was a tank on the desk with some coral and a dead goldfish floating at the surface. Norton wondered if he should tell the Warden his fish was dead. On the back wall Norton saw the rack of haggard shoes Choctaw spoke of. He felt glad that his shoes had not joined the group.

"I must admit," said the Warden, "the system of tunnels you boys laid out is impressive."

"You mean the system of tunnels *I* laid out," said Badger proudly.

"Yes," said Norton, attempting to divert blame, "Badger dug everything."

"How long did this take, Badger?"

"Two days."

The Warden slammed his hands onto the table. "I will not tolerate mockery!" He pointed out the window. Norton and Badger found themselves looking through the blinds. Hannibal was out in the yard, his teeth gnawing through a tree branch. They got the point.

"Sixteen months," said Badger, now speaking with a more humble tone.

"A shame all the work was pointless is it?" said Oslo, standing behind the Warden.

Badger sat silently in defiance. Norton then remembered Chub.

"You've got to be kidding," said the Warden after being told the predicament Chub was in. "You know something?"

"What?" Badger and Norton asked, coyly.

"It's on days like this that I love my job. I've built something I think you boys are going to like; been saving it for an occasion such as this."

*****

Not thirty minutes later, Badger and Norton found themselves being ordered into the courtyard. They were chained together at the feet. A rope was thrown over their shoulders and, as the residents of Dave Springs cheered for their bravery, Norton and Badger pulled a tall iron cage across the yard.

"They may cheer for you now," the Warden spoke into Norton's ear, "but when they see what you've become in a few days, they'll fear of your example."

Once they brought the cage to the middle of the courtyard, the Warden ordered that Oslo open the door and the escapee's enter. Badger and Norton did not realize how uncomfortable the cage would be. It's slenderness made sitting or kneeling impossible.

Norton watched curiously as a few of the residents were handed long metal rods. He wondered what kind of cruel purpose they would be used for, but was relieved when the Warden told the residents to poke around for Chub. Standing stiffly in the cage, Norton and Badger continually found themselves shifting their weight to ease the pain. They watched as the residents searched around the courtyard, poking the rods down into the ground.

The day went by and Norton began to lose hope. He thought maybe he would ask the Warden for permission out of the cage, if only to enter the tunnel to bring Chub some food. He then remembered that he too had yet to eat. On the second day, after the sun had risen and residents resumed the search for Chub, Norton started to think hard on where Chub might be located. He watched Choctaw wave at them gravely and then stoop over towards the sacred fire to send up a prayer.

"I bet that's where he is," he told Badger, "No one's poked around the fire." When one of the pokers was within earshot of the cage, he encouraged them to go check near the fire. The poker tried here and there and right up along the edge, but eventually looked over towards Norton and Badger and shrugged their shoulders. At noon the sun was directly overhead and their feet were beginning to burn. They would stand in the same spot for as long as possible but their legs were getting weaker and weaker. They kept altering their stance.

"I've only been acquainted with agony two or three times in my life," said Badger, "but this is one of those times." Norton knew what he meant. Their throats yearned for water and their bodies wanted sleep. They had been standing for over twenty four hours and awake for over forty eight. That night Choctaw snuck out and brought them a gallon jug of water which they gulped down in a fashion unlike that of which he had ever seen. He dug into the deer skinned sack that hung on his hip and gave them handfuls of candy to stuff into their pockets. They ate most of it then and there. This greatly renewed their strength and gave them a little hope, but by morning Choctaw was surprised to see them more exhausted than before. With their faces pressed against the bars and their bodies slumped in defeat, it was a tough thing to see.

Not long before noon on the third day, after all of the pokers except Choctaw and Otto had given Chub up for dead, a ruckus broke out across the courtyard. Norton was displeased at the sound, for it disrupted a mirage that was both beautiful and joyful. A white table had been before him, packed to its edges with turkey, fruit, cake and all sorts of eateries he had never seen. Off in the distance behind the great table, a field of green grass held a little pond where swans were swimming and playing gleefully.

"I found him!" A voice cried from across the courtyard.

Norton tried to push the sound out of his mirage. The swans were so graceful.

"Over here," yelled the voice again, "He's over here!"

Norton fought his way out of the mirage. Looking over in the direction of the voice he could see residents running towards Choctaw with shovels.

Badger and Norton watched as shovels of dirt flew into the air and the men doing the shoveling sank deeper and deeper. "Be careful," shouted Norton, worrisome that the men might hurt Chub with their shovels. The circle gathered around the diggers broke out in a loud hurrah and the men tossed their shovels aside. Together, they pulled Chub out of the hole. His body was limp and Norton feared for the worst.

"Water!" One of the diggers cried and it was brought to him promptly. Otto splashed Chub's face and then forced some of the water down his mouth. Chub gurgled then coughed and the circle began to applaud.

"Move!", said the Warden before anyone realized he was coming. Oslo jerked Chub up by the collar and led him over to the cage, but not without having to jerk him up twice more after Chub had fallen. Norton and Badger wondered if the Warden planned on having them rot before his eyes. That they could stand in the cage another day and still keep breathing seemed an impossible feat, but they did it, and on the morning of the fourth day, Oslo walked out into the yard jingling a set of keys. He unlocked the door, spit on them, then laughed as they crawled to their rooms, their legs being too weak to bear any weight.

*****

The next several days were spent in recovery. Badger, Norton and Chub had migrated over to Otto's room where he and Choctaw had set up beds to take care of them. Badger appeared to fare the worst. Otto believed he had pneumonia. Chills often swept over him and he continued to have difficulty breathing. When people asked how Badger was doing, Otto would reply, "Mean as ever." This much was true, of course. Badger was already making plans to seek revenge.

By the time the week ended, the three escapees were taking visitors and compliments. One elderly woman, in an act of admiration, even asked for their signatures. Badger and Norton responded indifferently to the woman, but the gesture lifted Chub's spirit to new heights. Most of the people who came in said something along the lines of, "That was a long time for anyone to be left out there. It's a wonder he didn't kill you!"

What stirred the men the most, though, were the few who came in and said there was talk of a revolt. "Some of the residents have been engaging in secret meetings," they would say, "A movement is stirring."

*****

When the men were well, Choctaw and Otto organized a communal gathering around the sacred fire. Every resident was invited, and by and large, almost every resident attended. Choctaw added extra wood to the fire and the residents hung around for some time. There was much clamour about the attempted escape and how it got under the Wardens skin. There was also talk of how Fran seemed to be coming around, finally beginning to remember his real name was Arnold Selenski, finally beginning to remember what the Warden did to him all those years ago. At one point the Warden himself even stepped out into the courtyard. He stood at a distance, watching from the main doors that led out of Wing B and into Wing A. Standing afar Badger could see the vulnerability in the Warden's eyes. Oslo stepped out of Wing A and could be seen shaking his head while speaking with the Warden. Badger imagined Oslo saying, "We can't stop the gathering, sir. We're out numbered."

The Warden went back inside and slammed the door.

Norton noticed Badger watching the Warden leave. He then spoke one word.

"Fire."

That word was all he needed to convey his thoughts. When Badger looked down at the burning wood before his feet, he knew what needed to be done. Norton could see the fire

reflecting in his eyes, and neither of them spoke another word.

CHAPTER FIFTEEN

Badger was standing before a map of Dave Springs that had been chalked out on the chalkboard behind him. His uniform was faded and his boots looked as though they survived two wars and an ice age. Across his heart one could see an array of medals. This was the first time anyone caught him in full regalia, and it was surely a sight to behold.

Norton and Chub had been enlisted to help him gather every resident in the home. A few of the residents were displeased with the awakening, but Badger's uniform cloaked him with an air of authority.

"In these trying times," Badger began, "one must strive," he pulled on every technique of oration he knew, speaking with intermittent pauses to enforce his speech, "with bravery, and strength, and courage of heart. If we are to break the shackles that bind us, we must act with solidarity and decisiveness."

"Solidarity and decisiveness!" called a man from the back, roused by the strong words. Everyone in the room could feel his sentiment.

"We were cast into this place individually, but when we leave, we will leave together. From here on out, we sleep, we eat and we fight as a team. I ask you to look to the man or woman on your right, and know that they are your brother or sister in arms. Without their help, you will rot behind the walls that encircle us now.

What I present to you, on this day, at this hour, is to be spoken in neither the hallways nor the latrines. What is spoken here shall be cloaked in secrecy. Do not let these words entire the minds of our enemy. Anyone who disobeys this order will be locked in the cellar and dealt with accordingly, understand? Good. I am glad you do." Badger's eyes looked focused and determined. "Know that in the following days, much will be demanded of you. There will be no sobby tears about what has to be done, no regrets about what memories of this place will be left behind, no doubts uttered in regards to the utility of our plan. We will go forth with confidence in everything we do. If we are making preparations and gathering supplies, we will do it in confidence. If we are shitting on the loo, we will do it in confidence. Every step taken and every decision made will be an action of confidence. This, ladies and gentlemen, is the mindset we must have.

What follows should be hitherto known as Operation Blitzkrieg. No doubt, over the centuries, armies have praised the swift and forceful style of attack, and on July the 18th, at precisely O' Seven Hundred, we will commence with a grand assault of our own. Albeit an escape plan, Operation Blitzkrieg is also a call to arms. For this is not merely an escape, but rather an act of war."

"An act of war!" yelled another man from the back, his walking stick shaking high in the air.

Badger pointed at the Chalkboard with a baton unsheathed from his side. "These points marked here," he said, tapping the board in various places, "are the locations of each fire extinguisher in the courtyard. If our plan is to have any hope of succeeding, they must be dispensed with. Hagrith, you and Martha will help Norton and Chub the night before the siege. They will be running around to dismantle all fire extinguishers and stow them away in the cellar." Badger began to assign everyone his or her duties and explain the plan. "Once in the cellar, you will then proceed to cut off the main water supply. I have already been down there to look. I can tell you ahead of time that there are three breakers that will need to be flipped."

"Otto, Choctaw, you two will be tasked with making a torch for each of the residents. And Choctaw, what do you think of fire arrows shot from the rooftop? We'll need to not only set Wing B on fire, but also Wing A if this is to work. Only an arrow can reach that far."

"It can be done," said Choctaw, gratified that he was called on for the task.

"You see," said Badger after speaking to each individual resident about their role in the plan, "by creating anarchy, the Warden and his staff will become disoriented and confused. Otto and I expect him to send a team of his staff into Wing B in order to escort us to the outside perimeter. From there, you can use one of the cars as a battering ram for the fence."

He stopped and stared off and away from the group, "As for me, I will stay back to take down the Warden."

When Badger finished, hands shot up around the room. Otto leaned in toward Norton, "Listen, in the history of Dave Springs Nursing Home, there has never been a Bingo Hall meeting so interesting as this."

"Nor will there ever will be," said Norton.

CHAPTER SIXTEEN

Frankie and Gomez entered the cafeteria with squinted

glances. Their shirts looked stained and dirty as though they

had been sleeping on the floor. Neither of the two had much

hair, but what they did have flared out unfashionably. Otto was

the first to see them enter the cafeteria, their heads stooped

low and their feet carrying them disoriented through the lunch

line.

"How many days has it been?" Otto asked, looking over at Norton who was also watching them.

"A little over two weeks," he said, "Is that all it takes? Two weeks?"

"You have to think," said Otto, "You get zero sun-light and just lay around on the concrete all day, listening to some twisted recording the Wardens made. Imagine it's loud and echoing off the walls, repeating over and over again?"

Not long after Frankie and Gomez sat down the Warden came marching into the cafeteria, dropping the volume in the room. Everyone seemed to be talking about something they did not want the Warden to hear.

"*Hic-uh-hic,*"

Everyone at the Norton's table turned towards Otto.

"Uhh-hic-uhh-hic,"

Norton and Chub exchanged a glimpse, then turned back to Otto.

"UHH-HIC-UHH-HIC," he grew louder and flailed his arms for something or someone to grab ahold of. Those at the table looked around, uncertain about what was happening. Soon, the entire cafeteria was looking in Otto's direction, a low ruckus of murmurs scattering around throughout the room.

"Is he okay?" A woman asked her friends.

"What's going on?" asked another.

Otto clutched at his throat, his hands forming the shape of a V around his neck.

"HIC! HIC!"

Norton shot to his feet, but only in time to watch as Otto's face plummeted into his porridge. The stubby bones of his spinal column were sticking out of the back of his bent neck. Otto was dead, dead like the cold moon on a cloudless night, dead like brick and mortar in a motionless wall, dead as in never getting up again or never speaking or thinking or employing any verb whatsoever.

The Warden walked over and, standing there for a moment, motionless over the body, gave what used to be Otto a stiff push with his index finger. The body flopped to the right, rolling out of the porridge and onto the floor.

"Somebody clean him up," said the Warden. "I'll have Oslo get the excavator and prepare the grave. Service is tonight at 6:00 p.m."

*****

Chub walked outside looking upward. He watched as planes traversed the evening sky, their white streamers long and tapering. *There are people in those,* he thought as a mocking bird flew down before him. He studied the way it rummaged through the clay pebbles on the ground, turning them over in search for something to eat. The bird would perch up every so often and tilt its head sideways to look at Chub.

"I've got dibs on the couch," said Norton.

Chub sounded off. He was loud and outraged, "What?"

"In case our next escape doesn't go as planned," Norton paused, "would be nice to have a couch."

"Our friend dies an' all you can think of is gettin' his couch?"

"I can't believe you would accuse me of only wanting his couch." Norton spoke defensively, "I'm hurt by it too."

By the time six o'clock rolled around everyone was gathered in the courtyard telling one of another of the memories they had with Otto. Badger scoffed at most of this, knowing the ones doing the talking were merely acting sympathetic. Grumpy wore some horrid mourning gown that made her look as though she teleported from the dark ages. Most of the women were wearing black, although, it seemed the men put little thought into what they should wear. Matter-of-factly, most of them didn't bother to change at all.

When the Warden showed, the group meandered lazily toward the cemetery. Once there, Choctaw stood up on a stool to deliver the eulogy. He wore a long khaki suite that flared out behind his thighs. Norton tried to place the year in which the suit might of been made, but gave up after thinking that a fickle thing to ponder.

"Our Father in heaven," Choctaw started. A few of the women could be heard giving a "*Shhh!*" to the others.

"Almighty and gracious God, our refuge and strength,"

Choctaw read not from a pamphlet as one might expect a preacher to use, but from a crumbled up piece of wide-ruled paper. "Grant us, we beseech you, a moment of silence for the great man before us." During the moment of silence, Choctaw pushed the crumbled up paper back down into his coat pocket and began to ad lib.

"Oh yes! Lord! Ancestors of old. Heed to our cries on this fateful day. One of our own has parted. He journey's into the underworld and the depths below, that great man before us."

Choctaw stopped and pulled his paper back out. "Uh, I'm sorry. I can't read what I wrote there." He paused, then remembered. "Right! Be ye therefore also ready, my fellow residents, for a day will come, when you too, shall journey to the under land. Arm yourselves to fight the fearsome Na Losa Falaya!"

Grumpy advanced forward and tore the paper from Choctaw's hands. "Heaven have mercy," she said discontentedly. "What's this talk of the underworld? Stop with the nonsense."

Choctaw was referring to an old Native American myth.

"This is madness," said Grumpy, "Let us sing a hymn and be done with it."

Choctaw surrendered the stool but not without some resistance.

The hymn that followed was hardly sung, as most of the residents stumbled through it underneath their breath. Apparently Grumpy was the only one who knew the words, and, before she finished, everyone began to disperse, going their separate ways. Norton and Chub stood up slowly, trying to figure out what had just happened.

"Even I wasn't expecting that," said Arm Pit. "Choctaw normally keeps it Christian and sticks to the message. Guess he's emotional over all this too... I think everyone's a bit shocked by this."

CHAPTER SEVENTEEN

Later on, Norton and Chub walked over to Choctaw's room in order to assist in the creation of fire torches. When they entered, Badger stood in the corner fiddling with the pieces of an electric fly swatter. Intrigued by this, Norton and Chub walked over to see what kind of shenanigans he might be up to.

Pow!

A protruding wire made contact with Badger's hand. He fell to the floor and grabbed his chest. Norton quickly got to his knees and gripped Badger by the shoulders.

"I'm okay. I'm okay," Badger repeated.

"What is this?" Norton asked, staring at the weird contraption the fly swatter had been turned into. The racket had been removed. All that was left was the handle and two prongs that were sticking out of it.

Badger lifted himself off the floor with a grunt. "It's a taser," he said. "I plan on using it to stun the Warden." He then unscrewed the bottom of the handle and out slid a battery pack. Sticking a voltmeter to the positive terminal, he got a reading. "We charged the batteries up to the point where they were about to explode. That test run was not intentional, but, I feel better knowing it works."

Choctaw worked his knife over a slender piece of wood. With gentle strokes, slivers peeled downwards until they began to curl away from the staff. "These maple slivers will burn slowly," said Choctaw, "Each resident should have around ten minutes before the end of their torch burns out."

At that instant a loud knock was heard at the door. Choctaw got up to answer it and in burst Arm Pit wheezing to catch his breath. "The Warden is coming," he said, and then sucked in deeply to refill his lungs with air. "Put everything away now!"

Choctaw scrambled back to the couch and began shoving the planks of maple under his sofa. Badger promptly threw the spare parts of the fly swatter into the trash and made way for the door. Norton, Chub, and Arm Pit quickly followed.

Once out in the courtyard, Arm Pit recounted hearing the Warden speaking with Oslo. "The Warden claims he can smell something brewing," Arm Pit let out. "He and Oslo are planning a search at nine."

Badger looked down at his watch, "It's eight forty. We have time to warn everyone, but we must move fast." With that the men split and began going door to door.

As they went around they were amazed by the number of residents gathered to make preparations. The early alert would prove to be a godsend. By the time the Warden showed up in the yard, all the residents had taken to their own rooms and resumed normal activities. This, however, did not lessen the effect of the Warden's wrath. Every room was ransacked. Thankfully, no one got caught.

Later that night, Hagrith and Martha went out to steal the fire extinguishers with Norton and Chub. Martha was the last to show up at the cellar doors. She clutched two of the extinguishers beneath her arms. Chub helped her set them down. He then proceeded to count the number they had gathered together, "Eight. Good work, that should be all of them."

"Right. Help me open these doors," said Norton.

"Why is there so much dirt?" Hagrith asked.

"This is where Badger brought all of the dirt from his tunnels. Here, let me see your arm, I'll help you down."

"I think I'm fine, thank you," said Hagrith as she stepped over the ledge of the cellar.

Norton and Chub followed behind Martha, flipping on a headlamp Badger let them borrow. This time they made sure the batteries were brand new. Chub found the breaker and gave the control panel a good scan. Norton flipped the switches that ran to the water supply. "Looks like we'll get four hours of sleep before morning," said Norton, "We're going to need every bit of it."

But Chub never went back to his room. Instead he went to the cemetery. The quaint tombstone came up to his knees, offering hardly any justification for what laid beneath it. He wonder over the life that Otto had lived when he was younger, wishing he had asked Otto more about his life before the home. Chub imagined the day Otto got his first car, the night of his wedding and every other milestone he could think of. He knew little of the life Otto lived, just as Otto had known little of the life he and Norton had together. Yet still, that didn't seem to dampen the connectedness between them.

The night was quite, the air clean, and the sky clear.
Each star dotted the sky sharply in the absence of moonlight.
Chub was particularly fond of nights like these, nights when
the Milky Way swept up from the southern horizon—it's
cloudy bands reaching out for space.

"You couldn't sleep either," came a familiar voice from
the dark.

"Didn't try," said Chub.

"I counted the tally marks on my headboard," said
Norton. "If we leave tomorrow, we'll have been here for a
year."

Chub brought his gaze from the infinite space above and
fixated on Norton. He chuckled.

Moments like this didn't happen often, but having lived
their whole lives together, they were not exactly rare, either.
The two spent their day without mentioning or even
considering the peculiar fact that tomorrow would be one year.
Their minds ran over the odds of escaping on the anniversary
of their acceptance, the very day they entered the home.

Could there have been something larger at work? Norton thought to himself, finding it striking that Otto would wind up with them for precisely the length of their stay, like some sort of guardian sent to guide them. *Don't be stupid,* struck across his mind. *You're being emotional,* he told himself, pushing this stream of reasoning away, his attention turning to the beauty of the night sky. "Such thinking never leads to any answers," Norton once told Chub. However, regardless of that, he could not simply disconnect from his feeling of connectedness to Otto now that he was dead. Nor could he escape from feeling as though he and Otto were meant to spend the small portion of life together that they did.

"We have nothing to put on his grave," said Chub, staring down at the emptiness that surrounded Otto's tombstone, his heart aching, "we should have prepared something."

Norton tried thinking of a place where they could go pick some flowers. He condemned himself for even humoring the idea. He knew there were no flowers in Dave Springs.

Turning, he scanned the cemetery over. A Marijuana plant had been placed on Old Man Parkin's grave, perhaps by one of the women when the Warden had his body reinterred.

Norton recalled Otto telling him they had another ceremony for Old Man Parkins while they were locked up in the cage. Chub watched as Norton walked over and grabbed the Marijuana plant, bringing it over to Otto's grave instead. The two stared at the plant for a moment, silent. Norton bent down and moved it over to the side of the grave a little more, thinking this to be slightly a better spot. Standing back, the two stared silently at the plant again, their heads turned sideways. This, strange as it was, provided a feeling of closure.

"That's better," said Chub, "I like that spot."

"Me too," said Norton, "And you know what?"

"What?" Chub asked, his voice wobbly.

"Otto liked Lemon Kush."

*****

"Wake up!", Chub nearly shouted.

"Uh... er, what?" Norton gruffed lowly, rubbing his eyes with the back of his hand.

"We fell asleep!"

The two had been laying down in the grass before Otto's grave. Judging by the level of his grogginess, Norton assumed they couldn't have been asleep for longer than two hours. When he finally managed to open his eyes the skyline was brightening. A deep navy spread downwards into a light blue horizon, leaving only three or four stars left visible for one to see.

"What time is it?" Norton asked.

"I don't know," said Chub, his voice frantic. "We need to hurry. We—"

"Calm down," Norton said, looking at his watch, "It's 6:45. We've got time. Operation Blitzkrieg doesn't start till

7:00." Norton thought about what might have happened if they didn't wake up in time, "Come on, let's head to the courtyard."

Other residents were beginning to step outside their doors, waiting for the clock to strike 7:00. They looked across the yard at one another, a few engaged in a series of encouraging nods and some held a clutched fist up into the air. The seconds ticked down until at last they began to walk over to the sacred fire. Torches lit, they each went back to their respective rooms. Shortly, a blaze could be seen in the windows.

After running the torches over the carpet, sofa, window linens and anything else that was fabric, residents began hurdling flaming chairs and coffee tables out into the courtyard. Norton and Chub soon found themselves standing by a small red box that wrote, "*FIRE,*" in capital letters, beneath which was an arrow and the words, "*Pull Down.*"

Norton rested his hand on the lever and stopped, "Wait," he said, "let's do it together."

Chub placed his hand on top of Norton's. The two gave the alarm a triumphant yank and a siren sounded across the grounds. A man could be heard broadcasting a yell over the deafening ring, "Burn it down!" Others followed up with chants of their own. The shouting formed an unintelligible noise of anarchy. Norton cast his view up towards the roof and observed Choctaw unleash a bath of flaming arrows. Chub and Norton jumped at the shattering of a window right behind them. Arm Pit launched rocks at every pane of glass he could find.

"Hey hey, ho ho where might the cocktail blow!"

They turned again, right as Wallie hurdled a Molotov cocktail onto the roof. When the bottle shattered and the alcohol inside met with the flaming rag, a pool of flame spread in a flash.

"Watch out," hollered Choctaw, barely dodging the flames. "I'm up here!"

Wallie ran to the other side of the yard and started launching from there instead.

Badger leaned with his back up against a wall. He was waiting by the doors that led from Wing A and into Wing B. As he hoped, the Warden threw open the doors and pounded his way forward. To the amusement of Badger, the Warden came by himself, as though he alone could quell the uprising. Badger snuck forward in a low stance, the makeshift taser in hand. Norton watch as the Warden shot stiff, falling to the ground like a plank of wood. Arm Pit hustled over to help with the tying.

"Now for the cage!" Badger cried. He then rallied a group by his side and a few moments later they were pulling the iron cage into the middle of the courtyard.

One in the group spoke up to ask, "You think the flames will reach this far into the courtyard?"

"No." said Badger. "But maybe they'll be close enough to cook him slowly!"

Arm Pitt held the honor of throwing him into the cage. Badger slammed the door forcefully and a round of residents walked by to spit on the imprisoned creature.

Norton and Chub ran into Wing A and came to a skidding halt when they realized the main entrance was on fire. "We'll have to find another way out."

They struck up the hallway and began searching for a door or window that might lead to the front of the building. By now the smoke was starting to accumulate at the ceiling and they were beginning to think their plan might have been overly done. Norton screeched to another halt. "Look what we have here."

A brick plaque sat above a door to their right, the word 'Warden' engraved deeply.

"Is it locked?" Chub asked.

Norton turned the knob and pushed the door open. The two expected to walk into a small room like their own, instead, they were standing in a great foyer lined with marble floors and accented by a grand piano rimmed in gold. Along the walls a massive mural of open tundra was brilliantly painted with lions, giraffes and a herd of wildebeest drinking out of a stream. From the ceiling a chandelier of emerald and ruby gemstones hung ornately. They were not standing in the Warden's room. They were standing in his house.

"This is amazing," said Chub, his voice filling the foyer with a crisp echo.

"Good acoustics," said Norton, noticing how the room amplified sound. Walking past the piano, Chub couldn't help but run his hands over the keys. A horrendous conglomerate of notes rang through the instrument.

The next area they entered was the kitchen. A large island with quartz countertop stretched out about eight foot long and the cabinets were intricately carved with geometric designs. Through a wide-open archway, Norton and Chub walked into what appeared to be a study. Bookcases were stacked full from the floor to the twelve-foot high ceilings. Chub walked up to the cases and read some of the titles. *The History of Incarceration: 1825 till 1950,* read one. *Through the Ages: A Treatise on Torture,* read another. Chub continued down the shelf he was on, *A Guide for Slow Death; The*

Handbook of Execution; Killing for Fun... as he continued, his gut moved further and further up.

On a desk in the middle of the room, Norton watched an ornament with a series of steel marbles that knocked back and forth, their repeated tink interrupting the silence in the room. One marble would fall and, coming to a standstill, would transfer its energy into the marble on the other side.

"I think it's called a Newton's Cradle," said Chub, noticing how Norton fixated on the steel marbles swinging from the sides of the ornament. "I've always liked those," said Chub, but, for some reason, he didn't like the one on the Warden's desk.

"This way," said Norton, heading to another door.

Norton and Chub thought the foyer was extravagant enough, but the room they walked into was unquestionably rich. The crown molding running around the floors and ceiling held a metallic sheen. Instead of the floor being ladled with tiles of marble as in the foyer, with Norton's keen eye, it looked as though the whole floor was a single piece of stone. Norton thought it must have been quarried out of a mountain and brought to Dave Springs on a train. No other form of locomotion, he thought, could move such a sizeable cut of rock. Scanning the floor over, he searched for a split in the grain where two pieces might have been pulled together. He could find none. The whole piece was continuous.

Chub, meanwhile, was staring at the un-miss-able monstrosity that stood tall by the foot of a bed. "How prideful must one be?" he asked, and Norton looked up to see a statue of the Warden. The statue was considerably bigger than the Warden in real life, which is not to say the Warden was small or short by any means, but merely that the statue was an exaggeration of his grandeur. Atop the head of this statue was a cowboy hat, fitted a little downwards toward the brim. In its mouth was a short stubby cigar that tapered and grew progressively fatter towards the end. His pants legs were chiseled in such a way to look worn and tuff and the boots on his feet were almost comically out of proportion.

What struck the two the most, however, was what laid across the bedspread. An electronic cash counter perched on one of the pillows and a grey briefcase sat opened wide.

"The briefcase!" Norton cried out and the two frantically started stuffing all of the cash back into it. A few bills were hanging over the sides of the briefcase and Norton struggled to get the lid closed. After bearing down with all of his weight, the clamps finally clicked shut.

Norton then swore himself and beat his fist into the bed.

"What... what is it?" Chub asked confused.

"We don't know the combination."

"Ah! Norton why did—"

"We'll worry about it later," he said. And with that he grabbed the suitcase and pushed on one of the doors at the back of the room, a lavish bathroom now gave way before them. Over the toilet a hazy window looked out over the parking lot. Norton stopped to scan over the bathroom in search of something heavy. He grabbed an electric razor off the sink and slung it violently. The razor smacked into the window but the only thing to shatter was the razor itself. He then

snatched the shower curtain down and tried using the rod as a

javelin. When this failed, Chub stole the briefcase and hurtled it

out the window. Norton swore yet again and jumped after it,

giving little regard to all of the broken glass. Chub moved

forward with caution.

"Over here," said Norton loudly; gesturing towards a red

minivan once the two were outside.

CHAPTER EIGHTEEN

"You still know how to do that?" Chub asked Norton, who was now under the steering wheel of the van, attempting to hotwire the vehicle.

"Awhir, awhir, awhir" the car moaned as it tried to start. "Awhir, rooompphhh!"

Chub reached his hand out to give Norton a high five but Norton failed to notice. He put the minivan in gear, reversed the front of the vehicle to face towards the gate, and then slammed into drive. He could barely believe it. Everything was going as planned. They were about to be free.

"Sayonara suckers!", he yelled out the window, right before they were flung into the floorboard. There they coughed up air bag dust and experienced flashbacks to the day they crashed their ice cream truck. Chub employed the use of foul language as Norton crawled up to look out the window and see the gate refused to budge. Norton threw the minivan into reverse again. This time he angled himself for different area in the fence. "Hold on," he commanded, charging the van over a small flag pole, two yard gnomes and a patch of shrubbery before the fence. Norton and Chub shouted in joy as the fence tore, giving way to their freedom.

The van rocked and bounced as Norton hit every dip and washout like they were ramps to be launched from. They had lost their front bumper during the collision with the main gate, and now they had lost their rear bumper on account of reckless driving. After around fifty minutes, the road started to smooth out and trees were springing up around them. Just as they were beginning to exit the desert, a dirt bike caught air from the ditch and landed in the road beside the van. Oslo was wielding a gun.

"The money," he yelled, "Now!"

Norton swerved off the road and Oslo's face could be seen tightening up for the fear of being ran over. He split left and geared down, pitting himself behind the van. Shots rang out and Norton grabbed Chub's head to cover it. With shards of glass splintering throughout the van, Norton unknowingly swerved back across the road, clearing a ditch and getting a sideways before finally swaying back up on what was now pavement. After the shots stopped, Norton stuck his head up to see Oslo still behind them. Bearing down on the breaks, the tires let out a squeal and the bike crushed itself into the back door. Oslo came flying over and onto the hood like a ragdoll. Norton then watched in the rearview mirror as Oslo tumbled down the ditch.

Further up the long stretch of road, blue and red lights were flashing defiantly. It was then that Norton and Chub remembered every resident at Dave Springs was court ordered, and by all accounts, they were probably considered convicts on the run. Hardened by this, Norton pressed down further, Chub watching as the speedometer crept upward.

When the police made out the vehicle barreling their way, they broadcasted the information to everyone dispatched.

"All units be advised, WT-7 has eyes on a suspicious vehicle... northbound on Rt. 221... red minivan... model unknown... stand by for further information."

As it got closer still, the officers realized the terrible speed at which the van traveled. Losing nerve, one of them pulled out of the way right before Norton and Chub sped through. Chub pulled his hands away from his eyes and let go of the passenger-side grab bar. "This is crazy," he barked at Norton and the two barreled onward, the police lights now somewhat distant behind them. They were hoping the patrol cars would be unable to catch up when out of nowhere, and literally falling from the sky, a helicopter swarmed overhead.

"*WARNING!*" came the broadcast; "This is the Phoenix P.D. Halt your vehicle now!" Norton laughed. The city's skyline was hardly far away. They could lose the helicopter amidst the buildings.

Charging onward, the helicopter tried to run Norton off the road. The pilot, however, kept parting way for the fear of a collision. Once in the city the helicopter rose high above the streets but, to Norton's dismay, still proved effective. Keeping eyes on the duo for as long as they could, the helicopter reported back to the ground.

A younger officer with high aspirations could hear them on the radio, "Moving west on 18th street. Unit six nearby."

"That's me," the young man thought, dropping his coffee as he sped off from the curb. Clumsy as he was, his timing proved perfect. In a daring attempt to stop the elderly duo, he managed to sideswipe the van into a violent fishtail. Now turned sideways, the van collided with a parking timer and sent change flying into the street. Norton and Chub hurriedly jumped out and ran.

"We're screwed," said Norton, "screwed!"

The young officer grabbed his radio before springing out of his car, "Perpetrators now on foot! Perpetrators now on foot!"

Just then, Norton noticed a truck driver helping a customer carry something up their apartment stairs. The back door of his truck was rolled open and, unwittingly, he seemed

to have left the truck running and unattended.

"The cargo truck!" Norton yelled, "Chub, hop in the

back!"

Purple words ran down the side of the truck saying,

'Murphy's Party Supplies'. Chub jumped into the storage cabin

and Norton ran around to take the wheel. They were off, but

not before the officer made an attempt to latch onto the back.

When his grip slipped, Chub gave a sigh of relief and looked

skyward to see if the helicopter was still on them.

"Look," yelled Chub at the top of his lungs. Norton could

barely hear him from the main cab. "The balloon!"

High on one of the buildings, a hot air balloon gleamed

in the sun. There was no mistaking that the balloon belonged

to Duffy. He had to be the only one in Phoenix who owned a

bright yellow and smiley-faced balloon. With renewed vigor,

Norton made sharp turns at every light and stole up a narrow

alley that Chub was certain they would get trapped in. When

they came through the other side the blue lights and sirens

were waiting and Norton had no choice but run through a spike strip.

All four tires were instantly shredded and the metal rims were grabbing at asphalt. Sparks glittered out behind the truck like streamers. The sound was horrendous. Chub was still standing in the back, the door wide open, an array of fireworks steadily being shot upon his command. He had used all the spinners and zingers when he spotted a rather large missile shaped tube, words on the side of which read *Grand Finale.*

"Holy Mackerels!" was Chub's involuntary response. Lighting the fuse he stood back, deciding it wise to cover his ears for this one.

"Kishhhh shaw!" screeched the rocket as it blitzed out of the truck, bouncing off the city street and ricocheting off a light pole. A burst of purple filled the air with the accompanying boom of a canon. This was followed by a series of dashing colors cracking into the sky, the end effect shattering windows out of buildings and leaving every pedestrian lying on the ground with hands over their heads.

"Sorry!" shouted Chub, regretting his actions, the firework resulting in more damage than he expected. His eyes now beheld a large black container at the back of the truck, white words on the side of which read *Fog Machine 5000.* Any repentant emotions he felt previously were washed away with elation, it just seemed so surreal. All of his life, he had dreamed of opportunities like this. Chub looked over the contraption, a perplexed expression on his face. There was a large motor on the side of the container with a red panel listing a long set of do's and dont's. Eyes bouncing from the instructions to the ignition key, Chub disregarded the warnings and turned the key at once. The engine slowly began revving up, a trickle of smoke patiently emanating from the mouth of the box. Chub was growing antsy, off in the distance he could see blue lights accelerating, the police were making up for lost ground, the *Grand Finale* having pushed them back a significant distance.

The machine let out a puff of smoke, then two more, "Puff", "Puff". Chub began laughing when the white balls turned into a steady column of smoke. They began pouring out from the truck like a jet stream, the sound no longer a series of puffs, but rather a consistent purr. "It's amazing..." said Chub with a choppy voice.

The blue lights slowly faded out of sight, disappearing somewhere deep within the whiteness. Norton rounded one last turn and split into a parking garage, atop of which was the balloon. Stopping the truck he got out hollering, "Chub. Leave it. We're leaving the truck!". Parking the truck in the entrance was Nortons way of blocking it off, but with the fog having engulfed the truck and everything around it, the police never saw them enter the garage in the first place.

"This way... arghh arghh." Norton coughed, ushering Chub up the on-ramp, trying to get out of the fog. Regaining some visibility, Norton and Chub made for an elevator in the distance.

As the doors closed Norton mashed number forty and

Chub

noticed the quiet serenading sound of a saxophone. There,

standing in that strange tranquility, they soared upward

towards the sky, postures taut and upright, feeling like

superheroes bound for the lair. The light bar above the doors

read, "37", "38", "39", "40". A resounding *"Ding!"* met their ears.

Several gusts of wind blew into the elevator. The hair left on

Norton's head blew back in triumph.

Norton and Chub were hesitant to believe what it was

they were seeing, their eyes having sent the signals faster than

their brain could process. Looming before them was an

especially colorful hot air balloon. Duffy hopped over the

basket rail, his motion graceful and lacking of age. In that

moment, neither of them was mindful of the current

circumstance, each of them flashing back to better days, they

ran towards each other, meeting in embrace.

CHAPTER NINETEEN

Norton and Chub helped Duffy loosen the ropes holding the balloon.

"Here, hurry," said Norton, "Get into the basket. I'll untie this last one."

Norton removed the final knot and ran toward the balloon.

"He's not going to make it!" Chub yelled.

Just then, Duffy dropped another rope for Norton to grab hold of. He dove for the cordage and, for a second, Chub and Duffy lost sight of him as he swung beneath the balloon.

"Climb Norton climb!" yelled Chub.

Norton looked down and realized the building was now twenty feet below him. Duffy could see the terror in his face as he struggled to pull upward. When Norton finally reached the baskets rim, they grabbed him by the belly and flopped him over the side. Norton stood up slowly, his gaze slightly disoriented.

"Put these on," said Duffy loudly, speaking over the roar of the engine. Norton and Chub found themselves looking down at the overcoats in Duffy's hands, but with the heat of the flame scorching their heads, they looked at the coats as if they reeked of some ungodly odor. "I'm serious," said Duffy, "It's going to get cold. When we get to forty thousand feet–"

"Forty thousand feet!" Chub broke out in a yell, stressing every syllable.

Duffy sent the hint of a smile in Chub's direction, then continued without hesitation, "You probably didn't know, but the world record for a hot air balloon is thirty thousand feet." His eyes were focused and looked determined. "Today, we'll make that forty thousand."

They were steadily accelerating upwards, as if the laws of gravity had been reversed. Norton and Chub noticed they were adrift and gliding sideways, charting out a similar path with the clouds. The city streets slowly grew smaller then faded from view. Their faces bore the look of someone receiving the outstretched hand of a stranger, neither of them having predicted that Duffy would come to their rescue. They stood still, observing the full weight of his loyalty, speechless as he diligently adjusted their oxygen masks and began fitting their parachutes.

At thirty thousand feet and still rising, they could see that the earth was no longer flat, its curvature spread across long sloping horizons. Through intermittent patches of clouds and the shadows they bestowed, rivers meandered towards vast seas of blue and a hundred hues of green were splashed across the land. An eerie darkness hovered above them, devoid of any hope and standing in sharp contrast to the oasis beneath them.

"Why did you come to our rescue? How did you know where to go? We haven't seen you in a year!" Norton exclaimed. His yell was slightly muffled by the oxygen mask.

Duffy looked amused, "Why friend, you were on the news," he said, his voice playful, reminiscent of the way he liked to jokingly speak. "My dog was scratching his rump, and I watching the *Daily Report*," said Duffy, fully aware that his comedic accent would have a calming effect. "I knew it was you as soon as the helicopter camera panned in on the windshield. When I saw ya headed to the city, I knew what to do." He paused for a moment, "Gents all over the world place'n bets on ya you know? High rollers too. From Bellagio Casino in Vegas to Sun City, Africa. Millions of greenbacks on whether or not you boys will escape." Jerking his posture straight he exclaimed, "Aye! They knew not what you would do. Take a hot air balloon? Never would they have guessed it. Modern day D.B. Coopers we are!"

They were imagining a room filled with professional gamblers, all of them watching the news, each of them placing bets on whether or not Norton and Chub would escape. "Two million says they won't escape!", howl's a man from the back, his hand up high with a betting card and a Rolex watch loosely wrapped around his wrist. Just then, a muttering sound can be heard from the far right of the crowd. Everyone turns to look and sees an older gentleman dressed in a long white gown, he is whispering fervently into the ear of a short woman, her head nodding attentively, and then turning to the auctioneer, "Make that five million from Mr. Ahmad Abdul!" The man dressed in white tugs sharply on her coat, whispering something else to her in Arabic, but just as she starts to translate for the auctioneer, he pulls her down to his ear again. The entire room holds an anxious gaze, counting each second, waiting to hear what this mysterious man has to say. "Correction!", says his translator loudly, jumping up and flailing her arms into the air, "For Mr. Abdul, that's five million waging they *will* escape! I repeat, five million that they *will* escape!"

What actually went down in casinos across the world, all that was lost or gained, they would never know, nor would they ever care. A mere week before, Norton and Chub were doomed for Dave Springs cemetery. With their eyes set on neon aurora toward the north and southern atolls toward the south, a serene peace swept over them and adrenaline no longer coursed through their veins.

"So thin... so fragile...", Chub said to himself, staring at an ethereal seam of white flowing over the earth, as if an angel's halo had been placed to protect it. He did not know he was staring at the atmosphere. Chub searched for words, desperate to describe what his eyes were seeing, "This is... life is–"

"Beautiful," said Norton, "Simply beautiful..."

Duffy and Chub found themselves speaking at the same time, desiring to say that same word themselves, the timbre of their voices resonating with the certainty that that which was said was true, "Beautiful." They spoke in synchrony, then they said it again, only this time, they whispered out of reverence. To be so mundane and commonly used, the word seemed foreign and new, as if neither of them had ever spoke it before, but instead, had spent their lives waiting, saving it solely for this moment in time.

Duffy killed the engine and the silence rushed in. Norton could feel his cheek being tickled by a tear. He did not wish to wipe it away or hide this small bead of emotion. They could see neither the empire state building or the golden gate bridge, yet this, this was the cause of the marvel they shared. All their toils and triumphs, their sorrows and cheers, their comrades and enemies, the mountains climbed and depths explored, all of it ceased to matter from their supernal view. That the spherical realm bore so many problems was hard to conceive.

Duffy opened the basket's gate and the men edged forward. With toes hanging over the edge and a sublime silence between them, a sound flipped and flapped out of Chub's backdoor. Duffy and Norton tightened their masks, glad they were about to leave the smell behind. Then, after one step forward, the men leapt into the embrace of Mother Earth.

*****

Oslo testified against his former boss and informed authorities of the loot Norton and Chub escaped with. The testimony reduced his sentence from 12 to 10 years. Further investigations revealed the Warden had ties to multiple cartels.

A 17-count indictment for charges ranging from trafficking to murder conspiracy gave him no hope for parole. Even with the first three floors of the 600,000 square foot production space burned, seizures by the Drug Enforcement Agency recovered more than 40 tons of yield. Dave Springs slammed the books as the largest drug bust in history.

Residents spoke out on the atrocities of the home, gaining public attention, which led to appeals for every Dave Springs sentence. Choctaw reunited with fellow tribe members. Arm Pitt resumed the peddling of moonshine. Badger returned home to join a veterans association. Frankie and Gomez were released but committed a series of crimes, ultimately being sent to a maximum-security prison. Once there, Frankie and Gomez were re-united with the warden. He was rather unhappy about his newfound love triangle.

The whereabouts of Norton, Chub and Duffy are peculiar to say the least. Three parachutes were found near Royal Arch in the Grand Canyon. Park rangers reportedly followed their footprints two miles south, but a violent thunderstorm forced them to call off the search. Backpackers

began looking in caves all across the canyon, hoping they might

sight the three bandits, or even better, find their loot.

News commentators proposed they could have kayaked

out on the Colorado River. A police officer testified that this

was plausible, making note of a call he received from a hiking

lodge for three stolen kayaks. The disappearance of three

kayaks seemed too obvious to be a coincidence, but a week

after they were stolen, three boys were found swimming near

the kayaks at the mouth of Bright Angel Trail. A local news

station filmed each of them apologizing to the owner of the

lodge from which they had stollen.

Rumors spread and grew plentifully as journalist

struggled to piece together how the trio managed to escape.

Some claimed they were hiding in the Alps, a travel brochure

for the mountain range having been found in what was left of

Chub's room back at Dave Springs. Others claimed they were

sipping pina coladas on some unknown island in the South

China Sea. Conspiracy theorists even went so far as to claim they were aliens from the Andromeda Supercluster,

accordingly sent down to gather Intel on humanity.

We may never know. As with life, some things are best

kept a mystery. Maybe the conspiracy theorists are right,

maybe the aliens are serving them a peace pipe. Maybe the

sands of white beaches lie beneath their feet. Maybe the snows

of higher peaks are beneath their skis. No one knows, and

guess what, that's okay. Every story will end, and in life, this

marks a new beginning.

About the Author

First, I would like to say thank you for reading this book. I have always felt as though everyone has a story in them. Personally, I feel as though I have been blessed with many. You probably have many stories inside of you too, although much like myself, there are probably some stories you intentionally choose not to tell. If I told you everything about myself, you might decide you don't like me too much, so I'll keep this section limited to my high notes.

I was blessed with a Tom Sawyer-esque childhood. Growing up near the historic site of a small trading post on the St. Mary's river, I would often swim from Georgia to Florida. This might sound like a long swim, but we could throw a rock across the line. In some cases, we even swum the rocks across (they were alligator eggs).

The town was known for the Okefenokee Swamp, or, as

the Natives called it, the *Land of the Trembling Earth*. Outside of a few tourists and some weird old men that had nothing better to do than watch a bunch of high schoolers play football, I never really felt as though I belonged. In hindsight, I fit in just fine. I wanted to leave as soon as I could, but the small town held its grip, and I slowly came to appreciate what I had there.

This small dot of the United States just so happened to be one of the few dark spots on the entire eastern seaboard. According to NASA, as well as my eyes, I was fortunate enough to grow up in a town where the heavens opened nearly every evening. As a result, there are several cosmic references in the book you have just read.

Currently, I am in the process of writing a non-fiction book that elaborates further on the cosmos. We truly are in a special place, and we are very fortunate to be here. The non-fiction book that I hope to publish is tentatively titled, *The Incomplete Guide to Life on Earth*. If you would be interested in learning more, you can see what I have copyrighted here:

https://zarymanning.medium.com/the-incomplete-guide-to-life-on-earth-6630a0d323b5

After graduating college with a degree in Anthropology, I hopped onto a gray hound bus with a close friend and left Georgia for Washington state. There, we would grab a plane to Anchorage, Alaska, and eventually fly out to Dutch Harbor where we would board a ship with some of the hardest working men and women that I have ever met in my life. Correction, to this day, these are the hardest working men and women I have ever met in my life.

While the deckhands fished for Pollock, my friend and I labored in the factories below. The experience was a hard one, and six days prior to our arrival back in Seattle, I became sick with a blood infection and a bought of nightwalking. No, I was not a Zombie, but more-or-less I became acquainted with paranoia and confusion the likes of which I would never wish upon anyone. They say at three days of zero sleep you start to hallucinate... this much I tell you is true.

Despite the living nightmare (as well as great inconvenience to my family and friends), I would say the experience was an overwhelmingly positive one (at least for me). If anything, it showed me to be grateful. It made me humble (if I wasn't already), it showed me hard work (something I thought I knew), and it opened my eyes to world outside of the United States. The ship cruised under the red, white and blue, but to this day, I can recall vivid conversations with men and women from many different parts of the world. Many languages were spoken there, and it was nice to see the union, even if there was some division. As Choctaw says in this book, we are all natives to the same universe.

Perhaps most riveting for me was the power of the sea. Not in the sense of its waves, but rather, in its tranquility. The sea provides far more oxygen than our rainforest, and we are ravaging it thoroughly. There was a camera on our trip, as well as a microphone, and I desperately failed at documenting both the seas plight and the seas glory.

After Alaska, I returned home and grabbed an apprenticeship with the United States Navy. Back on the St. Mary's, I had the honor to work on SONAR systems that US taxpayers have paid billions to obtain. Needless to say, somehow mother nature figured out a way to give these systems to whales and dolphins for free. A raw deal for the taxpayers if you ask me... but here we are. All of this was so that grown men could play soldier like when they were kids. And never mind the playground, the world is our stage now.

I bought and lived on a sailboat during that time. We gathered some footage of that too.... If I'm fortunate and blessed enough to live much longer, I might release a documentary about our oceans before I die. Hell, I might even finish the Incomplete Guide to Life on Earth.

Wait... finish an incomplete guide? The incomplete guide may never be finished I suppose... however, with your support, we might be able to get a little closer :--)

Follow Zary On

1. Medium.com

2. YouTube.com

Are you publishing house? Reach out to Zary through LinkedIn:

https://www.linkedin.com/in/zary-manning-4b8953198/

Zary is the author of *Elders on the Run* and *Network+ the Simplified Guide*.

He is currently working on a book that is tentatively titled *The Incomplete Guide to Life on Earth*, as well as a documentary about our oceans.

www.ingramcontent.com/pod-product-compliance
Lightning Source LLC
Chambersburg PA
CBHW021953170626
46808CB00001B/142